This bo... ...ld ... a ...

THE CHAPLIN CONSPIRACY

Stewart Ferris

Published by Accent Press Ltd 2018

www.accentpress.co.uk

Accent Press Ltd.
Octavo House
West Bute Street
Cardiff
CF10 5LJ

ISBN 9781786151858
eISBN 9781786151841

Thanks to Rat Scabies for agreeing to take a starring role in
this book:
www.ratscabies.com

For Leonardo

Friday 10ᵗʰ May 2013

Film purred through the sprockets of the projector at twenty-four frames per second. A lost and colourless world played out on the screen, waking a long-dead actor for a final performance. Decay was obvious to the nose and to the eye. An acrid whiff of sulphur. Stains that grew and shrank. There could be no doubt that this was authentic cellulose nitrate stock, which made it all the more difficult for those gathered at this private viewing to comprehend what they saw. Despite the deterioration of the reel, an anomaly was plainly visible. They had witnessed something impossible. Someone in the film belonged to another time.

The spool ended abruptly and the harsh white of the lamp revealed the true nature of the improvised screen: a creased bedsheet, stretched across the mahogany panelling in the drawing room at Stiperstones Manor. The tall man standing by the projector, Lord Justin Ballashiels, known to his few friends as Ratty, shrugged his bony shoulders. He looked at the rusty film canister on the table. The label gave no indication of the oddity contained within the footage. In an inky script, paled by a passing century, it simply said: 'Chaplin 1932'.

'Is it supposed to smell like rotten eggs?' asked Ruby Towers, leaning over the back of an itchy art deco armchair. 'And doesn't old film risk catching fire?'

Ratty tapped an ancient-looking extinguisher beside him on the parquet floor, failing entirely to reassure her.

'So what do you make of the film?' he asked.

'If I saw what I think I saw,' said Ruby, 'there's only one conclusion.'

'And that is?'

'The date on the film tin is wrong. It can't have been 1932. Let me look at it.'

Ratty passed the tin to her. She wondered if he had misread 1922 as 1932, but even so it wouldn't have made a difference. The stark and baffling anomaly would remain. She held the label to the light of the projector, but there was no ambiguity in the handwriting. The date was 1932 and it had not been tampered with.

'I don't understand,' said Ruby. 'It's a contradiction of reality.'

'Some clay-brained miscreant could have plopped this reel in the wrong tin,' suggested Ratty. 'But those clothes. The fashions. It has to be early 1930s.'

'And you would know,' Ruby said with a hint of mockery. Ratty had spent most of his life attired in the tweedy garments of his grandfather's era, but on the cusp of middle age he had recently taken the bold move of bringing his image in step with the current century. His ancestors would have been appalled by the denim and leather items that now dominated his wardrobe, and that new-found sense of rebellion gave him an agreeable feeling of wayward abandon.

'Reality is never at fault,' said a voice from behind a large Chesterfield at the front of the drawing room.

'Thought you were taking forty winks, Patient chappy,' said Ratty.

The Patient stood up in the white glare of the screen, sending a cloud of dust spiralling from the sofa into the light.

'As you must all appreciate, I am unfamiliar with the cinematic works of Charlie Chaplin. In a way, this remains the case, since this film is only a visual record of his vacation and was not intended for commercial release.' The Patient squinted through the brightness to see if he had his companions' attention. Sensing this was not the case, he decided to get to the point, but Ruby interrupted before he could continue.

'Have you seen *any* films or television before?' she asked.

'Well, no.'

'You haven't missed much,' observed Ratty. 'Hardly your fault, in any case. How long did that rotter keep you locked in his basement?'

'Forty-five years.'

'As long as that?' asked Ruby. 'Phew, that guy was a monster. What kind of father does that?'

The Patient fell silent for a moment. Ruby wondered if she had been insensitive. Tactfulness was not her thing. But if the Patient had the fortitude to cope with incarceration since birth in a concealed medical facility, interacting with no one other than his pitiless father – and only then in order to endure daily health tests to ensure he could provide spare parts for his twin brother, should they be required – she was certain he could cope with her crassness. Besides, his life hadn't been all bad, in her opinion. With access to a vast library and no other means of distraction during the decades that it took before Ratty was to cross his path and set him free, the Patient had become arguably the best-read person on the planet. She wondered if, in a small way, she envied the unique opportunity he had been given to devote so much time to books.

'The facts are undeniable, and we must work within them,' said the Patient, who retained his descriptive label even though it had now ceased to apply. 'We must follow the path of logic.'

'So we know Chaplin went to Europe in 1932,' said Ruby, relieved that the Patient was focussed once more on the mysterious film.

'And from my extensive reading on the subject, the Frenchman who appears behind him in the film could not have been present during Chaplin's visit to France in that year,' added the Patient.

'Because this impertinent fellow popped his clogs in 1917,' said Ratty.

'Precisely,' said the Patient. 'Therefore we have a conflict of two apparent realities. The reality of Chaplin's presence in France in 1932, and the reality of the French person's death in 1917. Only one of them can be true. Which one is incorrect?'

'There are plenty of news archives of Chaplin's visits to Europe,' said Ruby, trying not to sound as if she were lecturing her weary students. 'He even wrote a couple of books about his travels. He can't have been in France before 1917 because he was in Hollywood making films. And the war was on. France would have been a dangerous place. He might even have been enlisted to fight if he'd returned from America.'

'So we must consider the possibility that the supposed reality of a Frenchman's death in 1917 is questionable,' declared the Patient.

'What do you think, Ratty?' asked Ruby.

'Don't call him that, girl,' said the projectionist's mother, striding into the drawing room with a weighty gin and tonic in her hand. 'His name is Justin. Did your comprehensive schooling make such things too hard to remember?'

'Justin,' muttered Ruby, cursing silently at Lady Ballashiels' unceasing capacity for irritation.

'I'm ready to watch the film, boy,' said the old woman, placing her gin and tonic on a coffee table that had once supported a range of expensive nibbles during a visit by King Edward VII.

'My name's Justin, isn't it?' Ratty asked, winking at Ruby as he did so. His mother gave no response. 'And I thought you'd already seen it, Mater.'

'I once heard your grandfather talking about it, but I was never allowed to see it. They locked it away in the attic long ago. Probably been there since the forties. So rewind it or whatever you have to do,' she told him, settling herself into the Chesterfield next to the Patient. 'If you're serious about finding all that missing gold, it's entirely possible that the content of this film will give you an edge over everyone else.'

'I'd like to see it again, *boy*,' said Ruby, taunting her friend.

Ratty set up the reel once more. A fresh blast of the sour odour invaded his nostrils. He knew this was a type of film manufactured before such as thing as 'safety film' was commonplace. Proximity to the hot lamp of the projector had the potential to create ignition. He picked up the extinguisher and held it ready as soon as the movie started running.

'That thing's almost as old as me, boy,' pointed out his mother.

'Hush in the audience, please,' whispered Ratty.

'It's a silent movie,' said Ruby with unnecessary volume. 'And three people hardly constitute an audience.'

The actor in the film was clowning for his friends. This was a home movie, a record of Charlie Chaplin's travels in the south of France in 1932. Chaplin was standing on a windswept hill in front of a stone folly, waving at the camera. He pretended to pour a bottle of wine into his ear and puffed out his stomach as if it were filling up with *Pays d'Oc*. The camera panned clumsily to show the reaction of his companions, a forgotten entourage captured for a moment at the height of health and spirits: thumbs raised, smiles wide. The camera moved once more in the direction of the actor. The panning was smoother now, slow enough to show the details of the distinctive castellated folly. Pyrenean sun illuminated the stone turret and the arched window. Chaplin walked towards the camera using his trademark shuffle, feet splayed uncomfortably apart, his face and body starting to blur as the focus remained fixed on the stone building behind him.

A steel door opened at the top of the turret and a second man appeared. His face was visible. His features were familiar to those who knew his story. Moments later he returned to the interior of the turret, reappearing at ground level behind Chaplin. The camera focus changed, restoring Chaplin to clarity. The man from the turret pulled a shawl over his head as if to hide his identity, then passed closer to the camera, seemingly intent on a discreet departure from the scene. A gust of wind caught his shawl, however, and a frustrated and angry face now filled the shot before exiting to the side. The identity of that face was unquestionable. The square-set features, the dark eyebrows, the robust nose. He was the man who had paid for the construction of the tower. He was the priest who had become inexplicably wealthy after finding something during the renovation of his crumbling church in the late nineteenth century. His name was Bérenger Saunière. And he had died on 22nd January 1917.

Many thought he had died rich. Books had been written about Rennes-le-Château as the possible location of his reputed hoard of gold. Where hundreds before him had failed in their search for the priest's wealth, Ratty wondered if perhaps he could be the one to succeed.

Having no other income with which to maintain the sprawling edifice that was Stiperstones Manor, Ratty might secure the future of his estate with Saunière's gold.

The image on the makeshift screen bubbled and turned blank, then disappeared. A white flash engulfed the projector. The sprockets seized and the lamp died, replaced by a fierce tower of flame that almost reached the ornate ceiling of the drawing room. Ratty was prepared for this. Pulling the safety pin from the nozzle, he pointed the extinguisher at the inferno.

'Might as well pour neat gin over it for all the good it will do.'

'Hush, mother.'

'Ratty,' began the Patient, rising to his feet, 'your mother raises an interesting point with regard to the relative effects of water and alcohol in relation to the chemistry involved in the ignition of nitrocellulose—'

'Not now, Patient chappy. Just need to get this fire thingy under control.'

Ratty squeezed the handle and prepared to zap the fire. An unhurried stream of water fizzed into the flames and served to spread them further. The intense heat forced Ratty to stagger away from the projector. His spindly legs tripped over the power cable as he did so and caused the table on which the contraption was sitting to fall sideways. The Persian camelhair rug provided fresh fuel for the burning film. Flames spread to the nearest fauteuil, and then to the moth-eaten drapes. A first edition of *Hard Times*, tinder-dry from its years spent at the edge of a bookcase close to the constant breeze through an ill-fitting sash window, fizzed as its spine erupted.

'Told you there was something odd in that film, boy,' said his mother.

'Perhaps we could discuss it later, dear Mater. Bit of a flagration going on.'

'Just a little fire. Put it out!'

'There's no water left in this thing,' Ratty admitted, consciously having to raise his voice to be heard above the crackling noises.

'Oh, for goodness sake, Justin.'

'As I was saying,' shouted the Patient, moving swiftly towards the door and beckoning for the others to follow, 'water has no beneficial effect on fire of this type. In fact, it can make it worse. If we are to avoid the prospect of choking on noxious gases and our unconscious bodies undergoing baking and cremation, we must withdraw from here immediately. Let us learn the lessons of history, In particular I refer of course to the Dromcollogher cinema fire of 1926 in which nitrate film stock ignited and caused the deaths of forty-eight people, and we must not forget the Glen cinema disaster of 1929—'

'Calm down, Patient chappy,' interrupted Ratty, once again. 'You're getting historical.' He gathered his emotions with a deep and smoky breath, looking at the floor in shame. 'I must apologise to you, my friend. My brevity and impertinence are unforgiveable. And, of course, I agree wholeheartedly with your premise, so perhaps it would be propitious for us to retire to another part of the house? One that isn't burning with quite so much Hadean vigour?' He looked around the fiery room and realised he was talking to himself.

'This way, Ratty!' called Ruby from the corridor before the smoke in her lungs initiated a coughing fit.

***

The Marsaud family rarely celebrated together. Something always went wrong. As their brains filled with red wine, old tensions and disagreements would float to the surface. Bitter arguments would erupt, usually regarding the condition of the family chateau and whether the mediaeval fortress would even remain standing long enough for the younger members to inherit it. Only three rooms on the ground floor were now habitable. The remainder of the castle was derelict, capable of providing a home for nothing larger than bats and pigeons.

The sole human occupants were the current owners, known to the rest of the clan as *Grand-mère* and *Grand-père*. They consistently refused to consider the possibility of selling up, despite receiving frequent and sometimes eye-watering offers from wealthy foreigners desperate to own a part of the legendary village. This was not stubbornness. Moving away was not an option. They had a job to do and it necessitated confidentiality on a scale that excluded even their closest heirs. Meanwhile those in line to inherit the castle failed to help with the cash required for urgent repairs. The building was a problem, and with no progress towards disposing of the problem or fixing it, a prickly impasse lingered in their lives.

Today's celebration was unavoidable, however. Three generations were crammed into the grubby kitchen of the building that gave Rennes-le-Château part of its name. Fifteen souls in the same room, all overwhelmed with the same regret. It was the tenth birthday of the youngest member of the Marsaud clan, Maurice, which had necessitated provision of a fish stew, *bouillabaisse*. But the birthday wasn't the reason for the regret; nor was it anything to do with the noticeable increase in the rate of deterioration of the chateau. For once, the usual causes of conflict were absent. As they vomited and convulsed and flickered in and out of painful consciousness, and as *Grand-père* tried and failed to form the coherent words necessary to reveal something momentous to his rapidly fading son, they regretted taking up the offer of free catering from a start-up business run by two newly arrived American women.

'Guess we'd better get to work,' said Justina, tying her auburn hair into a pony tail as she stepped over the writhing body of a young man. 'You never told me how that stuff works. How long will they be out cold?'

'We can take our time,' replied Winnifred with a flat smile that stretched the wrinkles around her mouth and revealed teeth stained brown from a recent protein shake.

'Like a couple of hours before they wake up?'

'Wake up? Hah! They won't be waking up.'

'What are you saying?' whispered Justina with a tremble in her voice.

'I'm saying we can take as long as we want. The castle is ours. They won't be needing it.' Winnifred kicked the nearest body at her feet. There was no response. 'See?'

Justina dived down and listened for signs of breathing.

'No, no, no! You're kidding, right? This can't be happening!'

'It's already happened.'

Justina looked into Winnifred's eyes, scanning for the merest glint of humanity. She found no comfort there. 'What the fuck did you do, Winnifred? Sleeping pills in a fish stew. That's all you had to do! Fucking fish. Poisson and pills. That was all.'

'*Poisson*, poison. It's an understandable mistake. Serves them right for having a dumb language.'

'I didn't hire you to kill people!'

'You only hired me because I'm an expert at tunnelling. Sure, I get it – but I do things my way.'

'No, Winnifred, this is insane!'

'Look, you wanted me here because I tunnelled out of three jails, right? Why do you think they put me away to start with?'

Justina was sickened. Claiming her birth right had been an obsession for many years, but being party to mass murder was so far out of her comfort zone it seemed momentarily ethereal. Her feet no longer felt in contact with the cold flagstones beneath her. Reality had taken a wrong turn.

The ten-year-old birthday boy retched as he witnessed his relatives stop breathing one after the other. By the time his eyes closed for the last time, his entire family had been wiped out and their secret had died with them.

***

'You should have called us earlier, sir,' explained Denzil, removing his yellow helmet and unzipping the front of his protective coat. 'We might have been able to save more of your home. All we can do now is send a forensic team tomorrow to evaluate the cause and provide recommendations. Not squirting water on nitrate film will be top of their list, I'm sure.'

Ratty bowed his head like a scolded schoolboy. His mother stepped across a deflated hosepipe on the lawn and came to her son's defence.

'Now look here, young man,' she bellowed, dislodging soot from her shoulders with the power of her voice, 'I won't have some oik with five O Levels telling my son what to do. Justin did his best. At least he tried to put the frightful thing out. What did you expect him to do – phone you before the fire had even started? Give you enough time to finish playing rummy or darts or whatever ghastly pastimes you occupy yourselves with in the fire station? Perhaps if you'd driven a little quicker and got those hoses set up without so much faffing, we might not be in such a pickle!'

Denzil had already begun walking away before she reached the end of her speech. When he sensed the rant was over he turned back towards her.

'Considering they're knocking this place down next week,' he shouted to her, 'you should count yourself lucky that we even bothered to show up.'

'What rot,' she retaliated, flailing her arms theatrically. 'How can you spout such nonsense? Stiperstones Manor has been in the Ballashiels family longer than hereditary colour-blindness and Hapsburg chins. It will stand until the end of civilisation.'

Denzil ignored her and returned to his engine. Ratty walked backwards and managed to move several paces from his mother before the inevitable question erupted from her tongue.

'Boy, what's all this about knocking the manor down?'

'Nothing, Mater.'

'It's clearly not nothing if the local fire brigade knows about it.'

'I had a sort of letter,' he told her.

'A letter?'

'From the planning department chaps. Something about a new motorway bypass. They'll be here to flatten the place on Thursday.'

'What have you done about it?'

'Well, nothing.'

'Nothing?'

'You may recall, Mater, that I was recently busy in Spain trying to rescue you, prior to which I was somewhat occupied in South America trying to save the world. Administrative dealings with the planning department of Shropshire Council have not been my top priority.'

'Always an excuse, boy,' she said. 'It hardly matters now. The fire appears to have gutted almost an entire wing.'

'To be fair, Mater, it wasn't a wing that I was in the habit of frequenting. When I lived here on my tod I rattled around in the kitchen most of the time. The only damage in there is a trail of muddy bootprints from firemen chaps looking for a cup of tea. The library has survived, the turret is still hanging in there, and we should be grateful no one was hurt. I wouldn't be surprised if the smoke has killed much of the dry rot and choked the throats of the little woodworm fellows. So in a way, it's done us a favour. Well, for the next six days.'

Lady Ballashiels gave a vague acknowledgement to her son's logical thought processes before marching off towards a random fireman in order to give him a hard time about a subject she had yet to pick.

Ruby emerged from an unscathed side of the manor and collected mucky tea cups from the firemen as they packed up. She deposited the cups on a stone step and walked towards Ratty. 'Would you like me to contact the insurers for you?' she offered, licking her finger so she could wipe the soot stains from Ratty's forehead.

'Good idea,' replied Ratty, trying not to display his utter enjoyment of the simplest physical contact with Ruby. 'Been thinking about getting this place insured for some time.'

'I meant to arrange a claim.'

'A claim? Don't you need to take out a policy first?'

'You mean you don't have any insurance already?'

'This isn't one of those little semis you see littering the suburbs around the town, Ruby. Insuring a place like this costs an arm and a leg and if I paid those kinds of premiums every year I'd rapidly run out of limbs.'

'But you can't leave it like this, Ratty. That wonderful drawing room and the bedrooms above it are practically derelict. Plus there's the water damage in the cellars and the smoke damage in the hallway. Just restoring the blackened family portraits will cost thousands.'

'Remaining perched upon the family seat is ruining me,' sighed Ratty. 'Do you have any idea what those little men in overalls charge me just to repair a single Georgian window?' She shook her head. 'Nor do I, but I have more than a hundred of the rotten, draughty things. Windows, I mean, not men in overalls. Now, with the fire damage, I don't see how I can possibly carry on. I should just sell what's left of the manor and live in a yurt on a hill.'

'A yurt?' echoed Ruby.

'A tent thingy. That's how my noble family line will end up. Penniless yurt-dwellers.'

'It can't be that serious!'

'Ruby, you've known me since university. That's more years than I'm comfortable with. I've been broke the whole time, but I've scraped by. This crumbling manor is not exactly in showroom condition, but I've kept it standing. Well, most of it. You probably remember that time when the other turret collapsed. And parts of the gamekeeper's cottage haven't fared well. With a perennial famine in the tummy of the old piggy bank I could only patch up the holes and carry on. But this fire is too much. I'm beaten, old pumpkin. I can't believe it's come to this, but the family glory ends with me. The ancestor chaps would loathe and detest me.'

'I'm so sorry, Ratty,' she muttered, throwing her arms around him in a sympathetic embrace, fearing he might be about to break into a session of socially awkward tears. 'There's always a room for you in my flat,' she told him. 'But you'll have to leave the suits of armour behind. It's only got space for a single bed and a wardrobe.'

Ratty wiped some undignified moisture from his eyes and smiled at her. The scorched wing of his house was steaming like an overheated engine in the background, darkening the late afternoon sky.

'Infinitely appreciated, old moonbeam. You've always been there for me when it counted. You truly are the embodiment of something wonderful and in need of a body.'

'You'd do the same for me. It's what friends do. I'm just sorry I don't have more space to offer you than that little room.'

'It doesn't necessarily have to be that way,' said Ratty.

'It kind of does,' she replied. 'A bed and a wardrobe is the limit, I'm afraid.'

'I mean my role as custodian of the Ballashiels estate. It doesn't have to end with me. There is one possible solution.'

'No, Ratty, I'm not giving you a baby.'

'What? Hah! No. Goodness.' He blushed and adjusted his sleeves. 'I was referring to matters fiscal, not physical.'

'Again, no,' she replied. 'A treasure hunt is not a viable financial solution for you.'

'It would be if you helped me. And don't call it a treasure hunt. It's more than that. This is an archaeological and historical puzzle, and we can crack it. Together we would be unbeatable. We can do this. We can solve the Saunière mystery and bring home a mound of gold that would destabilise world markets.'

'I told you, it's a waste of time. There is no treasure. And even if that French priest did find some gold or any other source of money he would have spent it all in his lifetime. He was broke when he died.'

'Ah, but that's assuming that he really shuffled off his mortal wotsit when everyone thinks he did. We all saw his face. A tad more wrinkled than we've seen in the usual photos of him and the hair wasn't so dark, but we all agreed it was Saunière, right?'

'How can you be sure this film isn't already on YouTube for everyone to see?'

'Already checked on the Interweb. No one else knows. There were no other copies of Chaplin's home movie from France. And now it's been destroyed, no one else will ever have the advantage that we have.'

'Are you really still concerned about the contents of the Chaplin film reel when your house has just had a major fire? What difference does it make if Saunière was still alive in 1932?'

'Because,' Ratty began, his eyes suddenly alight, 'it meant he was up to something. And people only get up to something if there's money involved. In his case, I think there was more money down the back of his sofa than he knew what to do with. If he was alive in 1932 then he must have faked his death in 1917, and if he went to such extreme measures he must have needed to lie low with his loot. And if he returned to Rennes-le-Château in his old age, it must be because that's where he kept it. Do you see? It means he stashed his gold somewhere in that village. He kept it right there, underground, beneath everyone's feet. It's the rural mindset, you see. You're a big town girl, Ruby; coming from Guildford, you wouldn't understand the small village mentality that Saunière possessed.'

'What if I told you I wasn't from Guildford after all, Ratty?'

'Why? Is that the kind of revelation you're likely to utter?'

'I'm actually from a remote village called Bittenhurst. I know how country people think. Though, to be fair, most of my neighbours were stockbrokers who only came out to the country at weekends. Anyway, I've made my position clear that the Saunière treasure hunt is a waste of time, but if you really insist on pursuing this line of idiocy I can put you in touch with the greatest Saunière expert in the country. He lives in Brentford. I don't know if you'll approve of his taste in music, though.'

Lady Ballashiels returned to her son and his friend. 'Children,' she barked to the almost greying adults in her presence, 'why have you not asked me about the presence of the Chaplin reel in Stiperstones?'

'Good point, Mater. Why was that film in our possession?'

'I don't know,' she replied.

'Right,' said Ratty. 'Glad that's cleared up, then.'

'But did you know about your great-great-grandfather's liaisons in Paris with Emma Calvé?'

'Wasn't she the opera star with whom Saunière had an alleged predisposition for intimate anointments?'

'If that gibberish means what I think it means, boy, then yes,' said Lady Ballashiels. 'Your great-great-grandfather was involved with the same woman as Saunière.'

'Was there anyone in history that your family was not connected to, Ratty?' sighed Ruby. 'First Mengele, then Dalí, now Saunière. You lot certainly used to get about. One of the perks of having a house like this, I suppose.'

'I fear that period of influence will shortly expire,' Ratty told her. 'The council is about to demolish this place and build a motorway.'

'Nonsense,' laughed Ruby. 'This manor is listed. You can't knock down a listed property.'

'According to the council planning department's letter they can. All they have to do is compulsory doodah and grant themselves listed building thingummy,' he explained.

'But you can start a protest group. Organise a petition. Take the council to court!'

'Planners don't listen to protesters and petitions. Only the High Court can halt them now. And who will pay to take this case straight to the highest court in the land?' asked Ratty. 'As if the cost of maintaining the building wasn't sufficiently strenuous, I now have to hire a whole cricket team of lawyers to fight for my right to pay to maintain it. Now do you see why I need to find Saunière's treasure before the bulldozers arrive?'

'Sorry, Ratty, I don't want any involvement in this. It won't help you. It's a pointless distraction from what needs to be done. It would have been fun to hang around at Stiperstones with you for a while, and I don't mind helping with the clean-up here, but if you're heading to France to waste what little money you have left, I'll get back to doing some real archaeology.'

'I'm sorry you don't want to help me with my quest, Ruby. Your brains and my ground-penetrating radar would have made an unbeatable team.'

'Before you disappear off chasing wild geese, at least go and see my friend in Brentford to get up to speed on the latest theories and discoveries about Saunière. I know you don't have much time, but an hour with him could save you days of wasted effort.'

'What's the name of this giant of academia?'

'Scabies,' she replied. 'Rat Scabies.'

Saturday 11th May 2013

'Chisel?'

'Chisel.'

'Hammer?'

'I know. For fuck's sake.'

'So give me the shitting hammer, asshole.'

'Hammer.'

'Cover your ears, princess.'

'Don't call me that,' Justina replied, but her words were bludgeoned from existence by the clatter of hammer upon chisel. The sounds bounced in infinitely-decreasing echoes around the abrasive stone sides of the tunnel. Winnifred stopped.

'Drill,' she said, holding out her hand and displaying a bulbous and dusty bicep in the process.

'Drill,' sighed Justina, struggling with the weight of the tool as she passed it across. She paused for breath before adding, 'You were supposed to be a reformed character, Winnifred.'

'Bullshit. No such thing. Anyway, the locals bought your cover story, didn't they?'

'That we bought the chateau? I guess. But you can never really tell if they believed me or not. I couldn't sleep for worrying about it. So after we break through and split whatever's there, this is it. It's over. I'm leaving and I never want to see you again.'

'Suits me. Cover your mouth.'

The drilling was worse than the chiselling: unbearable noise mixed with suffocating dust. Again, Winnifred stopped. 'You think anyone can hear this?' she asked, pointing upwards, again revealing dirt encrusted muscles that threw imposing shadows in the torchlight.

'In Rennes? You're making enough noise for them to hear you in Wyoming.'

'I'm not stopping.'

'Me neither.'

Justina shone the beam of her Maglite through the debris in the air, picking out the texture of the wall that blocked their path. The sides of the tunnel were natural rock. The wall was brick. If men had built it, women could take it down. The gaps between the limestone blocks were thin and the mortar was strong, but the blocks themselves offered little resistance to modern tools of destruction.

'I think we're level with the wall of the churchyard,' declared Winnifred, 'and, if that's the case, there could be a crypt right on the other side.'

'Like I'd be putting up with all this shit if I didn't already know that?' came Justina's reply, followed by a bout of coughing to clear her dusty lungs. 'Just make a hole and find me some beautiful gold.'

'Crowbar?'

'What crowbar?'

'Give me the fucking crowbar!' shouted Winnifred.

'I thought you brought it.'

'Fuck. I left it in the castle.'

The women turned around. Winnifred pointed her torch to lead the way back along the tunnel to the dungeon beneath the castle where their journey had begun. The light picked out the shape of a stranger standing before them, blocking the passage. He wore a cream suit, and his shirt was unbuttoned to the waist as if to provide adequate light and air to the jungle of hair growing across his torso. In his hands he cradled a crowbar.

'Looking for this?' he asked, wearing a grin that appeared at once both charming and threatening.

***

'What did you say your name was?'

'Ratty,' said Ratty.

'That's a fuckin' shit name. How'd you get that?'

'On account of the conk,' said Ratty. 'How about yours Mr Scabies?'

'Call me Rat. Same thing. And I had scabies.'

Ratty stared at the man seated beside him at the bar of The Griffin. Rat Scabies was dressed in black trousers and an even blacker shirt, and wore the kind of boots that could enable the wearer to kick harder than a donkey. In fact, the former punk rock star wore an outfit that was almost identical to Ratty's, only somehow it seemed to suit him like a second skin whereas the aristocrat always looked as awkward as he felt. And right now he felt like he had wasted a day travelling to Brentford for this encounter. Could someone called Rat Scabies really be one of the foremost authorities on Saunière?

'So, *mon vieux batteur*, how did you become acquainted with my chumlet, Ruby Towers?'

'Guess she was keen on The Damned,' replied the drummer.

'I must profess ignorance regarding her Satanistic proclivities.'

'We met at a history conference,' said Scabies. 'I gave a talk about my hunt for the Holy Grail in France and afterwards she told me I was an idiot who should stick to drumming.'

'Sounds like Ruby.'

'I told her to fuck off,' Scabies added. 'We've been friends ever since.'

Ratty sipped his gin and tonic self-consciously. The lunchtime drinkers around him each had a pint glass in their hand and he sensed he was being judged rather harshly for his less than manly mannerisms.

'Charming hostelry,' said Ratty, instantly regretting his choice of words.

'Fuck that,' replied Scabies. 'I've met all the players in this game. The Saunière treasure's like a magnet, pulling in suckers from around the world. It's an interesting bunch of people, and some of them are really smart and they know their shit. But the only person who ever made a fortune out of Saunière's story was Dan Brown. No one ever dug up any gold or the body of Mary Magdalene or the Holy Grail. So tell me why you think you can crack this mystery when everyone else has fucked it up?'

'Gizmos,' said Ratty. 'Gizmos and brains. I have access to the brightest archaeologist in England and the whizziest ground penetrating radar scanning thingy known to science.'

'You know metal detectors are about as welcome in Rennes as one of my drum solos in a library,' said Scabies. 'And you can't even stick a shovel in the ground there without getting dragged away by the local *gendarmes*.'

'I appreciate that I may not look the type,' said Ratty, puffing out his insignificant chest, 'but I am no stranger to operating on the slightly questionable side of the law.'

'Ever killed anyone?'

'No, but I have a black belt in Pilates.'

'Finding whatever Saunière left behind can't be done without overlooking dozens of laws,' whispered Scabies, 'and you're not exactly a hardened criminal.'

'Fiddlesticks. I happen to drive an old Land Rover that's of doubtful roadworthiness.'

'So what do you want from me?' asked Scabies.

'I have absolutely no idea,' replied Ratty. 'Ruby seemed keen for us to meet. Frankly I'm beginning to suspect that she hoped you might dissuade me from this whole enterprise.'

'She wants me to tell you it's a fucking waste of time? She's right. Everyone involved in this has hit brick walls. There's no reason for you to be any different.'

'But did she tell you about Charlie Chaplin?' whispered Ratty.

Scabies shook his head and leaned closer. 'Go on.'

'I have,' said Ratty before correcting himself, 'well, I *had*, film footage that proved Charlie Chaplin visited Rennes-le-Château in 1932.'

'So what? The place has always attracted tourists.'

'But there was an anomaly in the film,' said Ratty. 'Something queer.'

'You mean like that mobile phone in a Chaplin clip?' asked Scabies. 'You're shrugging so you obviously don't have a clue what I'm on about. There's a film on a Chaplin DVD showing the scene outside a cinema in the twenties. Something to do with a premiere of one of his films. Anyway, there's this bird – or it could be a bloke, it's hard to tell – and she's holding something to her ear and rabbiting away as she walks down the street. It looks like a clunky cellphone from the nineties. Look it up on YouTube. People think she's a time-traveller or crazy inventor or something.'

'I'm sure it's most fascinating, but I can't see that it pertains to Saunière's activities. The fact remains that Charlie Chaplin visited Rennes in 1932 and the film he shot during his visit contains something just as impossible as that mobile telephone of which you speak.'

'So what did you see? An iPhone? A laptop? Time travellers from the future?'

'Saunière, Mr Scabies. We all clearly saw Saunière's face in a film shot in 1932.'

'So someone faked the footage,' said Scabies. 'There's a lot a fakery going on in the Saunière world. It's too easy to do these days. Anyone can fuck about with film using digital editing. Why don't you e-mail the video to me and I'll show you how they faked it?'

'Thing is, when I say footage, I really mean the kind of footage that can only be measured in feet. This was old film. It stank the place out. Then it kind of blew up.'

'Blew up?'

'Well, it sort of caught fire when I ran it through the old projector a second time. When I tried to put it out, it exploded and set fire to the drawing room. Half my house burned down.'

'Cool!'

'So I don't have the film now, but all of us recognised the priest. There's no question about it. He was definitely very much not dead in 1932.'

Scabies choked on his beer and stood up. 'Come on,' he said, heading for the exit to the street.

'Where are we tootling off to?' asked Ratty.

'France.'

'May I ask why?'

'To get a fucking croissant. Why do you think? We're going to find Saunière's gold.'

'Gosh.'

'Only kidding. I can't go to France, I'm playing a gig in Croydon tomorrow. But I think we should look into the idea of Saunière faking his death. I have some insights. I think I can help you.'

'It's awfully decent of you to offer your services, but I already have Ruby to help me. Well, I can call her up for archaeological advice when I need it. She doesn't want to get her hands dirty on this one. And there's Patient chappy. Not sure if he really wants to get involved, either, and anyway I prefer not to dilute the spoils.'

'So you just wanted some advice from me for free and you were going to keep everything?'

'No, no, no, no. Nothing of the sort. Absolutely not.'

Scabies leaned in close to Ratty's face. 'Really?'

'Well, maybe. Just a smidge. Though to be fair, you haven't actually provided me with any advice yet.'

'Bullshit. Of course I have,' protested Scabies.

'Such as?'

'Don't waste your time. Saunière's not gonna make you rich.'

'Ah, that. Much obliged, I'm sure.'

'This Chaplin shit. It might not bring you any closer to Saunière's loot, but it fits with some of the weird bits of the story. There's a photo of Saunière on his deathbed, right? It's in all the books, but it's not him. It's clearly some dead bishop geezer. So why did that photo ever get credited as being of Saunière? Easy. Because he needed an official deathbed photo as evidence of his demise. And there are rumours that he was fit as a violin right up to the day he supposedly died. Rennes is a hilltop village. It's a five mile hike to the nearest shops, and it's uphill all the way back. These people were fit back then. Saunière was strong. That's why I always thought he didn't die of natural causes in 1917. It had to be an assassination: Vatican or French government or something. But now I see it. He – or someone else – masterminded his disappearance. No one would look for him if he was meant to be dead. That would free him to do ...'

Scabies paused. He had no idea what the priest would do with his new-found anonymity and bucketloads of cash. Whatever it was, however, Scabies wanted to know. He wasn't going to let Ratty investigate this alone. 'You ever been to Rennes?'

'No,' admitted Ratty.

'You know where the tunnels are? You know whose palms to grease to get access to the crypt? To the graveyard? To the castle?'

'I must confess to being less than entirely *au fait* with those aspects of the mission as yet.'

'Do you know who the Knights Templar recently appointed to guard the secrets of the village? Do you even know where Rennes is?'

Ratty found himself pointing in a southerly direction, then retracted his arm.

'And do you have anyone on drums?' asked Scabies, with a wink. 'Come with me. There's more at stake with this story than you realise. Some unsavoury Herberts are going to come looking for you if they think you're close to sniffing out Saunière's gold. I've got some documents back home. You should take a butcher's. I think you need to know what you're up against and what might be unleashed against you.'

***

With the drill bit spinning at three thousand revolutions a minute and moving ever closer to his eyeball, Rocco Strauss was almost out of options. Handing over the crowbar and attempting to gain the trust of the two American women had clearly been a mistake. He hadn't expected to be so easily overpowered by the muscly woman, nor had he anticipated a fishing knife being held at his throat, and he lacked the strength to wriggle free of the duct tape that subsequently bound him. His attempts at reason and bribery and even seduction had failed hopelessly. All he could consider now was humour. He was not in a laughing mood, but it was the only way he could think of to defuse the tension.

'That's a masonry bit,' he told them through a dry and croaky throat.

'Huh?' asked Winnifred, pausing momentarily on the drill's route towards his face.

'It's perfect for tomb raiding, but for human flesh you're better off with a bit for metal and plastic.'

Justina and Winnifred glanced at each other. A flicker of a smile appeared on Justina's face.

'Don't even think about wimping out,' said Winnifred to her associate. 'We gotta see this through.'

'Come on, this is gonna be gross,' replied Justina. 'Don't you think we've caused enough harm? Let's just leave him here.'

'It will be really gross if you use the wrong bit,' agreed Rocco. 'A wood bit would be even worse, though. It peels the skin and muscle in long strands and it takes ages to clean the drill.'

'Don't be disgusting,' said Justina. 'And how come you know this shit?'

'Put the drill down,' Rocco whispered, 'and I'll tell you. And I'll also tell you anything you could ever want to know about Saunière's treasure.'

'He's bluffing,' grunted Winnifred.

Shit, thought Rocco. Even the old trick of pretending to know something so important that they needed very much not to kill him hadn't washed with these women.

'Wait,' said Justina. 'Let's see what he knows about this tunnel.'

'Who cares? It's a tunnel,' replied Winnifred. 'Let's get rid of him and carry on with the plan.'

'I think there's a chance we might miss out on some vital piece of information if we do,' Justina countered. 'Let him speak.'

'I can't talk with that drill pointing at me,' said Rocco. When the tool was lowered, he continued, trying to disguise the timbre of fear that shook the foundations of every word. 'This tunnel is contemporaneous with the castle and the church, built as an escape route for the castle's occupants way back when Rennes was a fortified hilltop town.'

'How long ago?' Justina asked.

'Between eight hundred and a thousand years. It originates in the castle dungeon and passes beneath the gardens of the intervening houses, finishing up in the crypt of the church. But the blocks that seal the crypt were installed more recently. My guess is that they were put there in Saunière's day, probably by the priest himself. They've been broken into a few times and rebuilt between the 1950s and 1980s. Since then this tunnel has come under the guardianship of the Knights Templar and no one has been allowed inside. No one, that is, until you two persuaded the owners of the castle to sell up, or so the rumour goes. Sealed the deal only today, I understand. I wandered in to congratulate you. I can't tell you how many people you've pissed off by getting the family to sell up. No one thought they would ever leave. With French probate law being what it is, no one thought the legal ramifications of ownership within the extended family would ever be resolved. But then, out of the blue, two American women show up with the keys and the deeds and start unblocking the entrance to this tunnel from their newly-acquired dungeon. Which begs a whole load of questions. If you have as much cash as it would take to persuade some very astute local French people to sell up and accept a Hollywood mansion in part exchange, according to my enthusiastically chatty sources, why do you need Saunière's money? And since you must know that this tunnel has been explored and re-sealed within living memory, why would you expect it to lead to any gold?'

'What do you mean, living memory?' asked Justina, trying not to sound deflated.

'Bullshit,' added Winnifred. 'There's a stack of gold behind this wall. There has to be.' She picked up the drill once more and squeezed the trigger so that it turned slowly.

'I do my research,' protested Rocco, leaning away from the drill. 'I'm not usually wrong. Unless, of course, you haven't bought the castle. And if you didn't buy it, then the owners are still here.' He waited for a contradiction, but none was forthcoming. 'That's it, isn't it? They didn't go to America. Everyone knows they would never sell. And they didn't sell it to you, did they?'

'If the crypt does turn out to be empty,' said Winnifred, 'I can think of another use for it. What do you say, Justina?'

'I don't understand,' she replied.

'If there's nothing behind this block wall because it's already been plundered many times before, like this asshole says,' explained Winnifred, 'then we should use the crypt for its proper purpose.'

'For depositing dead bodies?' asked Justina.

'Shit,' said Rocco.

'No one will go in there during our lifetimes,' said Winnifred. 'It could be a hundred years before the authorities grant permission to dig in Rennes. It's the perfect place to put them.'

'Them? How many are there?' asked Rocco.

'These rural French guys have large families,' replied Winnifred, 'and sadly they all succumbed to food poisoning during a birthday celebration. Serves them right for hiring American chefs. They should have stuck to local food. And now it's up to us to sort out the mess they left behind, and it seems that the crypt under the local church is where they would have wanted to end up.'

'How come you didn't see them on the kitchen floor?' asked Justina.

'I let myself in round the side. Through a window, actually, and straight down into the dungeon.'

'I reckon it's gonna be crowded in the crypt when we're done,' said Winnifred, looking Rocco in the eye, 'but who knows, maybe there's room for one more?'

Rocco thought about the warm spring sunshine radiating onto the graveyard just a couple of metres above his head. He wondered if he would ever see daylight again. Perhaps this kind of yearning for the simple warmth of life is what it was like to be dead and buried? Nonsense, the scientist within him decided. Being dead is just the same as not yet being born. Eternity passes in a flash. It was easy. Anyone could do it. Still, easy or not, he wasn't ready for eternity. There was one more thing for him to try.

***

The study in Scabies' attic rivalled Ratty's for the sheer quantity of books in the collection, but owing to a lack of space they were piled high on the floor rather than arranged neatly on shelves built by Georgian craftsmen. The only other difference was the presence of a drum kit in the centre of the room.

'No one else has seen this,' Scabies said, passing an envelope to Ratty. 'I didn't think it was significant before you mentioned the Chaplin reel, but now I see it in a new light.'

Ratty opened the yellowing envelope and withdrew the small sheet of paper. It was an invoice from a company in Paris, printed in French with a blotchy ink detailing the services rendered. Ratty couldn't make out what was written, but the name on the invoice was clear: B. Saunière. And so was the date: 1st November 1917 – almost a year after he was supposed to have died.

'Makes no sense,' said Scabies.

'There's simply no excuse for a sloppy hand when writing financial documents,' agreed Ratty.

'Not the handwriting, the name. If he'd faked his death by this time, why would he use his real name?'

'Golly. What a conundrum.'

'I've been thinking about this. First of all, maybe it's not the same guy. There might have been another B. Saunière alive in Paris back then. That's one possibility. Secondly, Paris is a long way from Rennes, so perhaps he didn't think anyone would know or care about his past. Thirdly, perhaps he was an arsehole and too stupid to think of changing his name. But I don't think it was any of those things. My theory is that without his real name he was nothing. He needed that name. It was his brand. It opened doors for him. It gave him power and influence.'

'To do what?' asked Ratty.

'People say he was into all sorts of shit. Voodoo. Politics. Blackmail. Murder.'

'Murder? Doesn't sound like the typical pastime of a village priest chappy.'

'1897,' said Scabies. 'Coustaussa. It's a neighbouring village to Rennes. The priest there was called Abbé Gélis. Someone bashed his brains out in his presbytery on Halloween night.'

'How frightful for him. Bet he wished he'd had a bucket of chocolates to give out.'

'No forced entry,' Scabies continued, ignoring Ratty's pathetic humour, 'no money taken, and this guy had moolah. Not on the scale of Saunière, but more than his salary would allow for. They never caught the killer, but the police report says that the body appears to have received extreme unction. That's the kind of crap only a priest can do to a dying geezer.'

'Gosh, are you saying Saunière might have been a naughty boy?'

'I think Gélis was on to him from the start. Saunière was paying him regular bribes for his silence. Then one night maybe Gélis upped his price and threatened to blab, Saunière got the hump about that and did him in with the fire poker. So yes, you could argue that he was into murder. When there's crazy money at stake, even a priest can get mean. Religion, politics and money can all make good people turn bad. Saunière had every motivation possible.'

Scabies produced another document from an envelope and passed it to Ratty.

'What's this fellow?'

It was a blank sheet of paper with a series of numbers written by hand in the centre.

'Could be anything, couldn't it?' asked Scabies. 'Phone number. Bank account. Emma Calvé's vital statistics.'

'Regardless thereof, how do you know it has any connection to the Saunière story?' asked Ratty.

'Because,' the drummer answered, 'it was found inside this.' He picked up a book and passed it over.

'A railway timetable?' Ratty leafed through it looking for more clues. Saunière's name was entirely absent from the pages. 'And how does this timetable link to anything relevant?'

'Because of the times of the trains,' said Scabies. 'Look closely. This is a timetable for 1917. The year Saunière supposedly copped it. Certain routes and times are underlined. If you follow the connections, it starts in Couiza and continues to Carcassonne, then to Marseille, across to Italy and up into Zurich. You're looking at the journey he made after faking his death. I didn't get it before you came along. I thought it was one of his villagers taking a trip to claim his dosh. Marie Denarnaud, maybe. But now I think it was Saunière himself; this is where he went in 1917. And that number is the key to his Swiss bank account.'

***

'I can help you,' cried Rocco.

'Bullcrap,' replied Winnifred, stuffing her torch into her pocket so she could drag Rocco's bound body through the hole she had created in the brick wall, bumping him insensitively over the loose rubble that lay at her feet. 'Anyway, you sound like a German.'

'You know there's no treasure in this crypt,' he continued, ignoring her observation. He was aware of a change of timbre in his voice. The space was wider, the ceiling higher, the temperature cooler. 'I knew that already.'

'You knew that because you heard me cursing when I broke in,' said Winnifred. She pulled out her torch and shone it at the walls. Justina climbed through to join them, and now twin beams of torchlight swung wildly around the space. The crypt was, as Rocco had predicted, empty. A sarcophagus chiselled from an unfeasibly large rock sat in the centre of the floor. Its broken lid lay in chunks all around. Coffin-sized recesses lined the sides of the room, designed to hold bodies but serving only as repositories of dust. Above was a vaulted roof of jagged stones. Ancient limestone blocks framed a doorway at the far end, now jammed with modern-looking brickwork similar to the wall through which Winnifred had just broken.

'I've studied this village in ways no one else has. I'm a scientist. My name's Rocco Strauss. Yes, I am

German. I work at the European Space Agency. I've got a doctorate in sciencey shit.'

Winnifred stood with her hands on her hips. 'Fancy university education, huh?' she said. 'This is tunnelling work. No amount of science is going to help down here. Now just shut your face while I decide—'

'Wait,' said Justina, pulling on Winnifred's sleeve. 'Let's hear him.'

Rocco didn't wait for Winnifred to respond. He went straight into his speech. 'I know why you've taken over the chateau. There are more tunnels under that place, but I don't think you know where to go next. I do. I know exactly where to look. I have access to satellites that can do the kind of shit you wouldn't believe. We've been developing the technology to find bunkers and underground missile bases, that kind of thing. The Americans wanted access to it to find Bin Laden – show them the extent of the Bora Bora caves – but these new satellites can also be used for cool stuff like orbital archaeology. It's not what we're supposed to use it for, because the money came from the military, but when you're in the control room on your own in the middle of the night with access to the coolest gadgets in the galaxy, well, you have to have some fun. Satellite archaeology is in its infancy, but I've run scans from orbit of this village. Highly illegal and could have cost me my job, but who gives a shit? So I've studied the heat signatures of this hill, I've seen the radioactivity readings and the rock analysis. The hilltop is like a Swiss cheese. Everyone looking for Saunière's treasure knows that. But I've seen inside the cheese. I know where the holes are. People tunnelled horizontally from the sides of the hill. They dug straight down under their barns, or sideways from underground rivers and sewers. The passages appear at every angle imaginable. Most of them are dead ends, abandoned probably decades ago.

Some of them connect. Others just miss their neighbour's tunnel by a few centimetres. People carried on digging well into this century, especially around the church. No one reached this crypt, but that doesn't matter because it's not the right crypt.'

Justina struggled to digest the mass of information she had just heard. Filtering the most salient point, she realised Rocco had revealed something of vital significance. 'What did you mean when you said this crypt wasn't the right one?' she asked.

'There's another. And some of the tunnels are pointing towards it.'

'How can there be another crypt?' asked Justina.

'This church isn't the original one.'

'Of course it is. This village only has about twenty houses. How can there be another church? We'd have seen it.'

'Right,' agreed Winnifred.

'I don't think they existed at the same time,' Rocco explained.

'Go on,' Justina said, leaning against the sarcophagus, enraptured by Rocco's revelations.

'The church above our heads – Saunière's church – only dates back about a thousand years. The village is far older, and originally there was a different church. It was located at the highest point of the hill. It's now a car park. One tunneller had the sense to head towards it, but he died shortly before he got his tunnel all the way there. Such a pity. Other tunnels also point vaguely in that direction, but they all fall short. The problem is the necessity to tunnel in secret. People had to start from their living room or their garage and dig down and then across the village. No one was allowed to start at the car park and dig straight down via the shortest route, so no one got there. I've seen the scans from the satellites. I know there's another crypt, and I know it's not been disturbed since Saunière's day. More importantly, I know how to find it.'

'Is he shitting us?' asked Winnifred.

'I would never consider doing such a thing to you,' Rocco replied. 'However, I would be prepared to help you move certain objects into this crypt, and to help you seal up the wall again in order that such objects will not be found for many years.'

'Objects?' asked Winnifred.

'Those poor people you murdered,' sighed Justina. 'Come on. Untie him with that terrifying knife of yours and make sure he understands that you know how to use it. We've got work to do.'

***

Ratty wished he had a photographic memory. The Swiss bank account number he had seen might be a repository of the wealth he needed to hire a dozen lawyers to bat for him against the planners at Shropshire Council, with enough to spare to restore the fire damage to his home and fix up everything else on his estate that was on its last legs. Maybe he'd even have change for a sizeable gin and tonic at the end. But his namesake had put the piece of paper swiftly away before there was time to memorise the sequence of numbers. He needed to stay close to Rat Scabies. Like it or not, he was going to have to team up with this drummer.

But could the Saunière mystery really be solved so quickly and simply? Just a short flight to Zurich, quote some numbers in each bank in turn until one of them throws open its doors, and walk out with a sack of loot? Things never usually went this well for Ratty. His excitement abated and he considered the matter more objectively. Scabies already knew this could be a bank account number. There was no reason for him to share this information. Ratty could offer no added value to any mission to claim the money. And that meant there was only one conclusion: Scabies had already attempted to do so.

'How much was in the account?' Ratty found himself asking reluctantly.

'Ah, I wondered how long it would take you to realise I'd already tried that for myself,' replied Scabies. 'Had a nice little jolly to Switzerland last month, as it happens. Very interesting result. I was told that the account was closed.'

'So there was nothing in it?'

'Fuck all. Someone had already emptied it.'

'What rotten luck. Just beat you to it, did they?'

'You could say that. They were actually a few years ahead of me.'

'How many?'

'The account was shut in 1931.'

'1931? Then there was never any hope for us.'

'The bankers wouldn't say who it was,' said Scabies. 'But, if what you've told me is true, it had to have been Saunière himself.'

'So he withdrew all of his lolly in 1931. Crikey.'

'That doesn't mean he didn't have wealth stashed in other places, of course,' said Scabies. 'He could have had other accounts, or he might have kept some of his gold stashed away in the tunnels and crypts beneath Rennes.'

'Which might explain why he showed his face there in 1932,' said Ratty. 'It's as if he was trying to gather as much money together as possible, building up to one big purchase. But what? A house? An island?'

'Or medical care. Or someone's silence. Or his life.'

'It would be beneficial if we knew where and when the fellow gasped his final wotnots,' said Ratty. 'That might help us understand what he was doing. But even if he continued to use his real name in Paris for a few months, it doesn't guarantee he was still using it in the thirties. Someone would have found a record of his demise if he'd stayed in France with that name, so either he changed the name at some point or he's not buried in his homeland.'

'He was sixty-four in 1917 when he officially copped it,' said Scabies. 'So by 1932 he'd have been knocking on eighty-odd. I wouldn't expect a big bloke like Saunière to make it much past eighty. So, although he survived the majority of the Chaplin era, on the bright side at least he probably never had to endure anything George Formby was about to impose upon the world.'

'So what now?' asked Ratty. 'Do we have any more leads, or are we at a dead end?'

'Your information about the Chaplin film has helped me understand more of the evidence. It's put it in a new context, and it's pretty cool, but you're right. We can't get any further without knowing more about Saunière's movements in his missing years. But it means we can start researching in an area where no one has looked before. No one has studied the documents of the twenties and thirties in relation to Saunière. It's virgin territory. You and me could make some serious progress on this, but you've got to keep it under your hat. We can't let word spread about what we know. You and me have to agree a partnership. We share what we learn. We split what we find. And we watch each other's backs. Right?' Scabies spat into the palm of his hand and held it out for Ratty to shake.

The aristocrat looked at the grey spittle proffered before him and considered his options. A deal with Rat Scabies was the honourable course, he realised. His visit had revealed a great deal about Saunière, and had proved that Scabies really was at the cutting edge of research into the subject. But that saliva. He grimaced and wondered if it was the custom in Brentford for all agreements to be made with such a disregard for hygiene. Best to get it over with, he concluded, dribbling into his own hand and clasping Scabies' with a firm grip. Like it or not, he was now in partnership with a rock star. He would have preferred Ruby as his right hand girl, but he was old enough to know that sometimes life threw you in unexpected directions. This sentiment was interrupted when Scabies ran downstairs to answer a persistent banging at the door.

'Probably an obsessed fan, or one of my stalkers!' he shouted from the hallway. Ratty detected a hint of pride in the statement. 'No,' continued Scabies, having opened his door. 'It's for you.'

Ratty jogged down the steps and joined him at the porch. 'Ruby and Patient chappy! What a delightful wotsit!'

'We have to leave,' ordered Ruby.

'But you've only just arrived, old veggie sausage.'

'Come and have a drink with us,' added Scabies.

'No,' said Ruby, 'something's happened and we need to leave.'

'Leave what? The house? The street? Brentford?' asked Ratty.

'The country,' replied the Patient. 'The fire brigade returned to investigate the cause of the fire at Stiperstones. They found a body. The police have issued arrest warrants for all of us.'

'Quite a dark horse, aren't you?' said Scabies, patting Ratty on the back. 'I thought you said you'd never done anyone in?'

'Of course I haven't. I'm sure it's a simple misunderstanding that a quick and friendly chat with the local constabulary will sort out. Constable Stuart is an old friend of the family.'

'No, Ratty,' replied Ruby. 'Stuart's gone. He's been replaced and there's a rumour that the new inspector is in league with the planning department and would like nothing more than to see you arrested and disgraced so that there would be no effective opposition to the road building plan.'

'Even so,' sighed Ratty, 'it hardly seems the gentlemanly thing to run and hide when we're all so obviously innocent. I think …' He paused for a moment. 'No, I definitely don't recall murdering anyone at home.'

'They haven't been able to identify the body yet,' explained the Patient. 'It's been badly burned in the fire. They said only scorched bones remained.'

'How thoroughly inconvenient for the poor fellow,' said Ratty. 'How did you get here if we're all under arrest?'

'Your mother tipped us off,' said Ruby. 'She's giving them hell at the police station, partly because I think she enjoys that sort of thing, but mainly to give us time to get out of the country. Once they've run proper tests on the bones I know they'll discover the skeleton has been there for years. It's the only explanation. No one will be too surprised to find something like that in such an old house, and then they won't have anything on us. But in the meantime you'll have been locked up or at least be out on bail with no prospect of foreign travel, and that means no chance of following the Saunière trail to the imaginary crock of gold that you foolishly think is waiting for you.'

'So I can't go home,' said Ratty, sounding moderately choked up at unwittingly becoming a fugitive. 'I don't suppose you brought my passport with you?'

'None of us did,' replied Ruby. 'There wasn't time. It doesn't make any difference because the ports will be looking out for us.'

'But Ruby, why would you want to flee when you know you're innocent?' asked Ratty.

'Because,' she sighed, 'even though your quest is an utter waste of time, I think, on balance, it will be far more fun to explore the south of France with you than to sit in a police station answering moronic questions.'

'And you're sure mother will be all right?'

'She's in her element, Ratty. Probably never been happier.'

'I know a geezer with a boat,' said Scabies. 'Well, it's not really his boat … but he's a geezer and he knows of a boat, if you know what I mean.'

Ratty shook his head.

'Do you want to get to France or not?' asked the drummer. 'Come on. I'll drive us to Hayling.'

'Will you come to France with us, Mr Scabies?' Ratty found himself asking.

'Of course. Wouldn't want to miss this adventure.'

'What about your gig?'

'My band needs me. My fans need me. But you need me more. So fuck them all.'

***

Mediaeval depictions of a hellish underworld with their imps and their flames and their tortured souls came nowhere close to the subterranean nightmare that Rocco endured for the rest of the day. Poetry and paintings could only stimulate the ears and the eyes, but a true Hades was something that pervaded the nose and churned the stomach. The gut-wrenching stench of death and its associated bodily excretions overwhelmed him, seeping into his pores and lining the insides of his nostrils. One by one, he dragged the bodies into the dungeon, through the tunnel and into the crypt where he attempted to lay them out with as much respect as his aching and nauseous muscles could muster.

Justina and Winnifred were not idle during this time. Aside from guarding the exit to the tunnel at the castle to ensure their prisoner did not harbour thoughts of escape, they took turns at scrubbing all traces of their victims from the floor and the furniture. Winnifred also gave some thought to the matter of the collection of cars in which the deceased family had arrived and which were now haphazardly parked in front of the chateau, in full view of the street. She peeled off her rubber gloves and grabbed the pile of keys that they had liberated from the pockets of the deceased.

'What are you doing?' asked Justina.

'I was thinking about the cars out front. It's weird.'

'I know, but what can we do?'

'Drive them out of the village. Maybe leave them in the parking lot down the hill.'

'Are you crazy? Leaving them in a public space will attract attention. At least here they're on private land.'

'So what are we gonna do?' asked Winnifred, throwing the keys back onto the table. 'Tell everyone we bought the chateau with the cars included?'

'The family is moving to the States, right? That's the story. It doesn't make sense for them to ship out their cars.'

'Mmm. Guess you're right,' grumbled Winnifred. 'We should go check on Rocco.'

'What for? I can hear him coming and going,' replied Justina. 'You really want to submerge yourself in that unholy aroma down there? Let him finish filling the crypt. I'm trying to figure out how we can use him without him double-crossing us. I don't trust him an inch.'

Rocco grunted loudly as he smashed a fallen brick against the sealed exit at the rear of the crypt. He had allowed himself several attempts at destroying this seal using the rubble at his feet after the laying out of each body. That way his movements from the crypt back to the chateau appeared regular and reliable. He wasn't sure if the sound of his efforts could be heard from the other end of the tunnel, so he ensured that each impact was at least partially masked by what he thought was the kind of noise he might be expected to make if he had trouble lifting the bodies into the nooks at the sides of the crypt.

He was making progress, but it was insufficient. The eighth body was now laid out, and his escape plan had dislodged three bricks. At this rate the hole would still be too small for him to climb through by the time he had laid the final body to rest. He needed a way to accelerate his progress. There was also the matter of what was behind the bricks. He wasn't sure. It looked like wood panelling or plasterboard and, so long as there was nothing built up against it on the church side, he was confident he could kick his way through that layer. But he would never get there unless he found either the time or the tools to speed up the demolition process. He considered using the small torch Justina had provided, but it was flimsy and anyway he could do nothing without its light. He needed the crowbar, or some other piece of solid metal, and that meant taking a huge risk when he returned to the chateau to drag away the next victim.

He had already taken a break three bodies ago. His request to use the bathroom had been granted, since it didn't present an escape risk: the window was jammed, tiny and overlooked a precipice that fell away more than sixty feet down the steep, rocky side of the hill. But Winnifred wasn't as stupid as she looked and sounded.

She had frisked Rocco when he collected the next body, ensuring he hadn't secreted a length of pipe or some other item that might potentially help him to break out of the crypt. So Rocco had believed there to be no chance of obtaining anything from the chateau that might be of assistance. Only now he thought otherwise. Winnifred would pat *him* down again, he knew, but she wouldn't think of groping the stained and putrid clothes of the elderly lady that he was going to collect on his next trip.

The walk back through the tunnel was worse each time. Grooves had appeared in the dust on the floor, carved by the lifeless legs of the people he had dragged, and now the dust was congealing into lumps and stains where unsightly fluids had spilled from their hosts. Rocco stepped through the doorway into the dungeon. He looked around for signs of the crowbar or anything that could perform a similar function. The squalid room was devoid of content, comprising nothing but the limestone blocks from which it was constructed, tinged with a hue that glistened as though the walls were alive.

The spiral stairs spread the echo of his laboured breathing as he climbed.

'He's back again!' called Justina.

Rocco was used to this routine now. Whoever was guarding him would watch him closely and report his comings and goings. He reached the top step. Justina was waiting for him in the draughty corridor that led to the kitchen. The remaining bodies lay here already, waiting in turn for him to take them down.

'I really need some water,' gasped Rocco, exaggerating his state of exhaustion, though not by much. 'Just a little break.'

'Winnifred! You hear that? You got water for him?'

Winnifred appeared from the kitchen with a glass of water. 'How many left to do?' she asked him.

'I think there are seven more,' he replied. 'It is very physical work. Perhaps if I could be permitted to sit and rest for a few minutes?'

'Sure,' Justina replied. 'We're not monsters. You're doing great work, bud.'

Rocco eased himself stiffly onto the floor of the hallway, adjacent to the row of bodies. Opposite was a table on which sat the crowbar, the hammer and the chisel. Justina returned to the kitchen, Winnifred was still cleaning and decontaminating, rendering the crime scene spotless, working in a methodical way that suggested this wasn't her first time. Neither woman paid attention to Rocco as he sat, sipping his water and contemplating his next move. He could see the knife that Winnifred always carried, strapped menacingly to her waist. Its serrations and curves glinted at him in the dim light, threatening to disembowel him at the first opportunity. He sensed Justina was not only in charge, but far less inclined towards violence than her associate. However, he wasn't convinced he could take advantage of her weakness; a brute force escape via the crypt was still his best option.

Or was he being stupid? It suddenly occurred to him how utterly idiotic he was being. The tunnel to the crypt was the only one accessible from the dungeon, but it wasn't the only tunnel beneath the chateau. He had seen three others in the orbital scans. One led down to a water course and offered a highly discreet method of escape. The only question was where in the castle did it originate? If not from the dungeon, perhaps from another cellar room or a hidden staircase beneath a turret?

He considered a risky dash to the derelict corners of the chateau in the hope of finding the entrance to the preferred tunnel, but was paralysed by second thoughts. It was a flawed plan. He didn't know the layout of the castle. If he even found another passage it would be bricked up at one end or the other. No, he had to grab the crowbar and hide it in the clothing of the old woman who was next in line for his funereal services. The second Winnifred's back was turned, he did precisely that, before announcing his intention to return to work and inviting her to frisk him.

'Not this time,' she replied, unwilling to touch the unsavoury stains that by now covered his clothing.

Rocco dragged the body down the spiral steps, carefully holding the crowbar in place to ensure it wouldn't fall out and crash loudly down the staircase. At the foot of the stairs he spread the body out on the steps so as to cause an inconvenient blockage to any pursuers. Not an insurmountable obstacle, but an unpleasant and unwelcome hindrance nevertheless. With the crowbar firmly in hand he sprinted along the tunnel to the crypt and turned the bricked up exit into rubble within minutes. The layer behind the bricks did indeed turn out to be plasterboard, and a few whacks smashed a ragged hole through which he could squeeze. Behind this hole were stone steps, rough-hewn and steep, leading to a trap door above his head. He climbed a few of the steps and reached up. The texture of the door proclaimed its antiquity: rough oak planks braced with cold, black iron. He pushed hard. It refused to move.

Attacking the trap door with the crowbar had no effect. It was as if an almighty weight stood upon it. Then he heard something: a voice in the tunnel, Winnifred's angry tones bouncing around the walls. Rocco turned off his torch and pushed upwards with all the force he could muster but the trap door remained secure. He glanced down at the hole in the brickwork that led back into the crypt. In the blackness he saw, at first, nothing. Then a hint of silver shot through the space. A blade, cutting the darkness in two. He deduced that Winnifred was climbing through from the crypt and there was no indication that Justina was around to mitigate her violent streak. Winnifred's torch brought the base of the stairwell into dazzling relief. Rocco blinked rapidly, and the slashing of Winnifred's knife took on a strobe effect as she advanced through the hole and up the steps towards him. With adrenaline surging through his muscles, giving him strength the like of which he had never known before, Rocco lined up his fists for one more push.

***

Charlie's pockets were bursting with souvenirs. Not the official kind that tourists were sold in the museum gift shop, but the real thing: priceless, irreplaceable artefacts from Saunière's domain. He was standing in the priest's 'secret room' at the side of the church wondering what to steal next when the floor beneath his feet began to vibrate. It was most disconcerting. He wondered if he had been spotted climbing under the rope barrier across the nave of the church and letting himself through the unmarked door which had led in turn to this tiny and peculiar space, barely larger than a closet. Had security officials activated a defence system designed to punish errant visitors? It was unlikely. The church contained three security cameras, feeding through to monitors in the ticket office by the gift shop. He'd seen those monitors: none of the cameras was working. He had nothing to worry about.

But the banging beneath his feet didn't stop. He looked down and could see the outline of a square hatch in the wooden floor. For someone of his generous proportions, entering such a trap door was not an option – Charlie was not designed for squeezing into tight spaces – but someone must be down there and it sounded as if they wanted to come out. He stepped off the door. The hatch flew up, carrying with it, on a wave of unstoppable momentum, the unexpectedly odorous Rocco Strauss.

'What happened to you, man?' asked Charlie, recoiling from the maelstrom of foul smells that seemed determined to invade his personal space. 'You been checking Saunière's sewers or something?'

'Quick! Close it! Stand on it!'

Charlie did as instructed using only one hand to close the hatch in the floor, the other being preoccupied with the need to squeeze his nostrils tight. 'I gave up waiting for you in the restaurant,' he said. 'They didn't sell donuts and I was getting bored. Had to get my reserve stash from the van.'

'Those American women who bought the chateau – turns out they didn't buy it, just murdered the owners. And now they're after me,' Rocco panted. 'We need to run to your van. On the count of three. Ready? One, two—'

'Hey, wait a second, dude. You're not coming anywhere near my wagon smelling like that.'

'Charlie, this is life or death. Those women are crazy.'

'Women, huh?'

'No, Charlie. Don't even think about it.'

'You get yourself cleaned up. I got this.'

'She has a knife, Charlie. She's an escaped convict. She's not going to be charmed with an offer of a stale donut. We have to leave Rennes. Now!'

'Well you're gonna ride at the back in the bathroom and as soon as we get down to the river I'm throwing you in.'

'Whatever, Charlie. Let's just get out of this madhouse.' Rocco pushed at the small door that led out of the secret room. It didn't move.

'Push harder,' said Charlie, his feet once again sensing forces trying to lift him off the trap door. With three hundred pounds of body weight on his side, not to mention the various stone and metal items that bulged from his capacious pockets, he wasn't going anywhere until he was ready.

'It's stuck!' shouted Rocco, now putting all his weight against the door, to no avail.

'Did you think we would just let you go?' called a muffled voice.

'Is that you, Justina?' asked Rocco.

'I wanted to apologise for the way you've been treated,' she replied.

'Er, right. Can we go now?'

'I am a researcher, like you, Rocco. I came here, just like you, intending to solve a mystery, that is all.'

'But, unlike you,' Rocco replied, 'I didn't choose a psychotic killer to help me. My associate is an obese university dropout with minor kleptomaniac tendencies. You might have to lock up precious artefacts when he's around, but he wouldn't hurt a fly.'

'A fly? Sure I would,' protested Charlie. 'But not a lizard.'

'I know,' said Justina. 'I've made a big mistake. She's not my friend. She's just an expert at digging tunnels. Things got completely out of control as soon as I started to trust her. Now I'm scared and I want out.'

Rocco heard a scraping sound as Justina dragged away whatever item of furniture she had been using to block the door. The door opened. Justina stood before him, palms open, submissive and saddened.

'This one of the chicks, huh?' asked Charlie, noting that the vibrations beneath his feet had ceased.

'I want to get away from Winnifred,' explained Justina. 'She scares me. I didn't poison that family – that was her doing. I just wanted them drugged for a couple of hours so we could check out the secrets of their castle. Winnifred went too far. I covered by telling the guy in the souvenir shop opposite that we'd bought the place and sent the family to America, thinking that would buy us some time. Then you showed up and I panicked. I didn't know what to do with you. Please, Rocco, you have to believe me.'

'Donut?' offered Charlie, reaching into a pocket and producing a paper bag that sprayed sugar dust onto the floor as he pulled it open.

***

The yachts of Hayling marina gently throbbed on the pulse of the sea. Ruby gazed at the neat rows of gleaming white sailing yachts and the sexy motor boats with an instinctive expression of disapproval. Most of these expensive toys probably stayed put in the marina for fifty-one weeks of the year. It was the kind of decadence she could only dream of.

'Which one is your friend's boat?' she asked Scabies.

'I'm waiting to hear from him. Don't know if he's decided yet.'

'Why do I get the feeling that we're heading away from lawfulness?' she sighed.

'Need I remind you, Ruby,' said Scabies, 'that you're already wanted by the police and are on the run. If you happen to hitch a ride in a borrowed vessel, it's not gonna make things any worse for you. Let's just get ourselves to France, spend a few weeks getting pissed and climbing into caves and graves, and by the time we get back the whole Stiperstones skeleton business will have been sorted out.'

A phone buzzed in Scabies' pocket. He looked at the message.

'Well?' asked Ruby.

'He says it's the white one.'

'But they're all white!'

'Just kidding. It's a motor boat called *Dumpling Stew*.'

'*Dumpling Stew*? Doesn't sound very fast,' she mocked. 'Anyway, which one is it? I can't read all the names from here. Why doesn't he show us?'

'Well, as it turns out, he's not going to be able to join us,' said Scabies, 'but he assures me *Dumpling Stew* is fuelled and ready and capable of getting us to Normandy. And more importantly, he's left the keys on board and filled the fridge with sandwiches. Top bloke.'

'There's the old girl,' said Ratty.

The others looked at where he was pointing.

'What, behind that floating rubbish dump?' asked Ruby.

'Sorrowfully not, old sea salt. Can you see the name on its side?'

'Ratty, the whole boat is almost on its side. It's listing horribly. And what's it made of?'

'Plywood, by the look of it,' Ratty replied.

'Yes,' added the Patient. 'It was the common boat construction material of the sixties and seventies, from which era this craft appears to date.'

'So,' said Ruby, 'it's made of soggy, leaky, old wood. Might as well be made of sliced bread. And every other boat in the marina is made of glass-reinforced plastic that never rots. That tub wouldn't even make it out of the harbour. Why can't we take a different one?'

'You want to pay to hire a legit boat, Ruby?' asked Scabies. 'You'd have to show your passport and prove you're a competent skipper.'

'Beggars can't be wotsnames,' pointed out Ratty.

The four of them approached *Dumpling Stew*. Scabies gave it a nudge. Its lines creaked. He unzipped the canvas that covered the rear of the open cabin and climbed aboard. The deck creaked too. 'Come on. We should go before we miss the tide,' he called.

'Is it about to turn?' asked Ruby, climbing aboard with delicate steps.

'Is what about to turn?' asked Scabies.

'The tide.'

'How the fuck should I know? It's just the sort of crap sailors spout, that's all.'

'So does anyone here have the foggiest about seamanship and navigation and all that flimmery-flam?' asked Ratty as he became the third person to make the deck groan under the unfamiliar weight of passengers.

Ruby and Rat Scabies looked at each other and shook their heads. Then they turned expectantly to the Patient.

'I think I can be confident of delivering us to Cherbourg before dawn,' he declared, still standing on the floating dock.

'Before Dawn? She got a slower boat, then?' quipped Scabies.

The Patient looked at him blankly. 'I was referring to the length of the sea crossing, which from my recollection of the charts of this part of the world amounts to about ninety nautical miles, taking us six hours at an average velocity of fifteen knots, so if we leave just after sunset we would arrive—'

'You sailed before?' interrupted Scabies.

'No,' the Patient replied. 'I don't recall ever being this close to a boat, let alone piloting one, but I am fully versed in the theory of yacht skippering and navigation by the stars and mechanical engineering and the rules of the sea. It also happens to be the case that I am well read in matters of seaworthiness and timber rot and the statistical chances of a boat such as this suffering a catastrophic failure on a voyage of this length.'

'What are you suggesting, old seadog?' asked Ratty.

'I am suggesting that you forget about travelling to France on this craft,' he replied. 'I studied the sea conditions in the forecast pinned to the door of the clubhouse. A weather front will pass by soon after the sun sets. We are going to encounter winds up to force six. If you allow a margin of error in the prediction and assume it could be as bad as force seven, the stresses on the structure of this old wooden boat would be too great. One wave hitting the beam would split the boat at the seams and send us to the bottom of the ocean before we knew what was happening. And I can see that there is no life raft on board. This boat is not equipped for use out of sight of land.'

Ruby, Ratty and Scabies re-joined the Patient on the dock.

'So how the fuck are we getting to France?' asked Scabies.

'We have the greatest chance of success against an agitated sea if we take the largest vessel available,' the Patient said, pointing at a gleaming, seventy-foot superyacht.'

'Wow,' exclaimed Ruby. 'But we don't have the keys to it.'

'Or the sandwiches,' pointed out Scabies.

'I have a rudimentary knowledge of nautical electrical and security systems,' said the Patient. 'This yacht has two engines, a life raft, enough mass to ride a force ten storm, and, if it has sufficient fuel in its tanks, then I suggest we take it.'

'That's frightfully impressive, Patient chappy,' said Ratty, 'but do you think there's a possibility that we might attract a tiny amount of attention from the *Gendarmerie* upon our arrival?'

'I have already considered that scenario,' the Patient replied. 'This yacht has a tender capable of seating all four of us. We must drop anchor a kilometre off shore and take the tender to the beach. No need to get anywhere close to a marina or any officials.'

'I'll get the sandwiches from the floating death trap,' said Scabies. 'You get that gin palace fired up. I hereby appoint you captain, Mr Victim or whatever your name is. Deal?' He spat in the palm of his hand and held it out for the Patient to shake.

'Patient,' replied the Patient, looking with curiosity at the palm offered to him. 'Without immediate recourse to sanitising products I would prefer—'

'We should hurry,' interrupted Ruby. 'Looks like someone's coming.' She pointed at two men walking purposefully from the marina car park towards the floating docks. 'It might be nothing, but just in case.'

'Shit,' said Scabies, wiping his hand on his backside. 'Forget the sandwiches. Everyone on the gin palace.'

'Hey!' shouted one of the men, now running towards the yacht that they had yet to steal. 'What are you doing?'

The Patient busied himself with a set of wires he had extracted from the cockpit panel. Ratty untied every mooring line he could find. In seconds the yacht began drifting in the light breeze away from the dock at a tangent that created a gentle impact with its neighbour. Considering the slow speed of the collision, the two yachts created a deafening screech as their fenders proved inadequate and the hulls stressed and scraped against each other.

'Stop!' shouted the angry man, now standing on the jetty just feet away from the drifting boat. 'That's private property!'

The other man jumped onto the neighbouring vessel and ran around to a point from where he could jump aboard the stolen craft.

'I say, Patient chappy, any joy with those engine thingummies?' called Ratty.

In lieu of words, the Patient replied with the sound of cranking engines that quickly began to tick over smoothly. As the man on the neighbouring boat steadied himself for the leap, the Patient pushed the twin throttles to half power and the yacht surged away from the dock. The man had committed his momentum to a point of no return and found himself hurtling into the frothy sea that the yacht had, only moments before, occupied. The passengers steadied themselves against forces that tried to topple them as the Patient lurched the boat into a tight turn and accelerated towards the open sea and the rapidly setting sun.

'Good work, Patient chappy,' said Ratty. 'So you deduced that this craft has all the fuel we need to take us to the land of baguettes and body odour?'

'I did not,' replied the Patient. 'I estimate that we do not have enough to take us even half way, but I also deduced that leaving the marina swiftly was more important than waiting to be caught. However, I can take us back if you prefer.'

The calm shore lights shrank behind them and the sea loomed dark and lumpy before them. The Patient weighed up his options, sensing that no one else had a clue which way to go. Returning to the marina was pointless, but they needed fuel. All other marinas would be alerted to the boat's theft and hence they wouldn't be able to obtain fuel anywhere. They couldn't reach France in this boat and they couldn't refuel it. The answer became obvious.

'An offshore sailboat mooring,' he announced. 'We need to find a sailing boat moored to a buoy and transfer ourselves over from this yacht. Then we can sail to France and glide silently to a remote beach.'

Ratty, Ruby and Scabies shrugged. They were out of options. The evening air was freshening and the wind was picking up. In the distance a helicopter cut through the sky towards them.

'That the police?' asked Scabies.

'Let's not hang around to find out,' replied Ruby. 'Full speed ahead, Captain Patient.'

'I recommend the opposite,' he replied. 'Abandon ship. Everyone into the tender.'

'Why do you keep changing your mind?' Ruby asked.

'Because if that is the police coming after us it may well be the case that this yacht has an automatic alarm and tracking device fitted. The police will know our location all the time we are on board. If we launch the tender, we will be untraceable. Of course, the helicopter might be nothing to do with us, but I do not think we should wait to find out.'

***

'Well ain't this nice,' said Winnifred. 'Decided to defect, huh?'

'Put the knife down,' whispered Justina.

'Right, so we're suddenly all friends and these guys who we know nothing about are just gonna forget about the bodies we put in the crypt beneath our feet? I don't think so.'

'I'm Charlie,' the obese young man stated, offering a sugar-encrusted hand in welcome, seemingly oblivious to any threat Winnifred might pose to his safety.

'Fuck you, fatty. Come on Justina. Get your shit together. We gotta deal with these guys and get back to work.'

'I told you we're splitting. We're not partners any more.'

'Well that's just a bit too damn convenient, ain't it? Let me remind you of something. You brought me here on the promise of a half share of enough treasure to buy me a goddamn island. We break into one crypt and already you want to quit? Well that's not acceptable. We're a team, and we stay a team until we find what we came for. If killing these bozos makes you uncomfortable, we can tie them up in the dungeon and make use of any information they can give us.'

Charlie stepped forward, putting his vast bulk between Winnifred and Justina.

'Careful, Charlie,' said Rocco from the back of the tiny room. 'She's got a knife.'

'That's not a knife,' chuckled Charlie.

'Don't get cocky, Charlie. This isn't a movie,' Rocco continued. 'You haven't got a bigger knife so don't even think about going there.'

'Sure, I haven't got a bigger knife. That's true.' He reached inside his trousers and produced a gleaming sword three feet long. 'This is better than any knife, I reckon.'

'Where the hell did you find that?' asked Justina.

'It was on the wall in the museum. I think it's a Templar sword or something. I didn't think they'd miss it.' He thrust it menacingly towards Winnifred.

Winnifred backed off and closed the door between her and the others. 'How do you know you can trust them?' she shouted from behind the door. 'It only takes one of them to call the cops and we're screwed. They might even *be* cops. We can't take that risk!'

'And how can I trust you? You're turning crazy, Winnifred! You scare me!'

'Can I offer a suggestion, ladies?' asked Rocco.

'Shut up in there!' Winnifred called.

'No,' said Justina, 'go ahead.'

'We are in a tricky situation,' Rocco explained, speaking loudly so that Winnifred could hear him on the other side of the door. 'I understand that. Circumstances dictate that mutual trust is a problem, but that doesn't mean we shouldn't try to solve it. As I've already explained to you, I'm a scientist. That means solving problems is what I do. So this is what I think. If we fragment and fight, it can only harm our prospects. Treasure hunting is difficult as it is without having someone trying to sabotage our work. It's even harder when we're worried that someone is trying to kill us. It therefore follows that if we can find a way to work together, we will have a better chance of success. All of us. Pooling our ideas and energies and talents will get us to Saunière's secrets faster than working against each other. Think about this, Winnifred. I have no desire to spend my time in France giving evidence to the police, spending months talking through a translator in a trial, trying to get you locked away for what you did. Horrific though it was, it wasn't my business.'

'Horrific, huh?' asked Charlie.

'You don't want to know,' replied Rocco. 'I propose that the four of us work together until we find what we're looking for, or until we decide that the time has come to give up. Only then will we go our separate ways. No one will talk to the police in that time, or afterwards. We can only benefit from this approach. Any other course of action will harm the interests of us all. Think about it. I broke into the chateau in the first place. Reporting your crimes will only incriminate me, too. Charlie stole a sword and probably anything else that wasn't bolted down in the museum. Why would he go to the police? We're all potentially in trouble with the law, to greater or lesser degrees. The more we dig the more trouble we'll be in. That puts us all on the same side – the wrong side of the law. That's why I think we can work together. So Charlie, you put that sword away. Winnifred, you put your knife down if you haven't already. I'm going to open the door and we're all going to shake on our four-way partnership.'

Rocco squeezed past Charlie and turned the door handle. He pushed it a little, enabling him to peek at the other side to check if Winnifred was still holding the knife with intent to harm them.

The knife was absent.

He pushed the door further.

Winnifred was also absent.

'You must have bored her, dude,' said Charlie. 'I knew you should have left her to me.'

'Shit,' said Rocco. 'I thought I had resolved the situation. You think she heard any of that?'

'Guess not,' said Justina. 'I hope you can remember that speech because it sure would be helpful if you can get Winnifred to listen to it. But until she does, we're in danger. We should go somewhere she can't find us.'

'How about we find a tunnel that goes close to the other crypt?' suggested Rocco.

'Close? Isn't there one that takes you all the way into it?' Justina asked.

'Probably not any more. Obviously I think Saunière had access to it via a tunnel, but there's nothing showing up on the scans. I think he filled it back in with the same type of rocks and soil as the surrounding area. That's why I couldn't see it. People have dug separate tunnels since Saunière's day, but we'd need to find the best one and finish it. We're going to get dirty.'

Charlie and Justina stared at Rocco's filthy attire. There was no need to comment on the irony.

'Where do we find the best tunnel to start from?' asked Justina.

'Follow me,' said Rocco, leading them out of Saunière's secret room and into the gloom of the church, keeping an eye out for Winnifred all the while.

Outside, they walked along an unlit street to a souvenir shop. It was filled with books about Saunière's life and legacy, DVDs, and pamphlets about the Templars and the Cathars, esoteric and new age trinkets and novelties, postcards and branded pens. With no customers inside, the manager – an elderly woman sitting on a stool at the rear of the shop – was beginning to cash up for the night.

'The best tunnel is under the floor of this gift shop,' said Rocco, pointing inside. 'I'm going to ask if we can see inside it.'

'You can't go in there,' said Charlie. 'Look at you!'

Rocco looked down at the blood and excreta that stained his clothing. Charlie was right.

'Can I wash in the back of your van and borrow some clean clothes?'

'I guess,' said Charlie, handing him the keys without enthusiasm. 'The water tank is full. Just don't touch anything until you've got that shit off you.'

'We'll wait inside the gift shop until you come back,' said Justina. 'It'll be safer than hanging around on the street.'

Rocco joined them ten minutes later smelling fragrant and wearing clothes that would have better suited a hippo. 'You have a tunnel under this floor,' he said to the shopkeeper.

'It is just there beneath your feet,' she replied in a heavy Languedoc accent. 'I'll put the lights on. You'll be able to see it better.'

They looked down at the thick glass plate on the floor. Beneath it a rocky passage had been hewn vertically into the ground. It made a pleasing novelty feature for the shop, a reminder of the chaotic history of the village.

'May we see inside your hole?' asked Rocco.

Charlie sniggered like a kid.

'You already can,' the shopkeeper replied.

'I mean, I would like to go down there. Would you mind?'

'It's not possible,' she replied. 'You need a torch and a rope, and in any case when you get to the bottom there's nothing there.'

'If we could provide our own ropes, would you mind if we go down there?' asked Rocco.

'It is still not allowed.'

Rocco reached into his wallet and produced twenty Euros. 'Would this help?'

She adjusted her reading glasses and leaned in close to look at the money before commencing a fit of gesticulation and shouting. 'What are you doing? You are a crazy man! You cannot bribe me! Get out!'

Rocco put the money back into the wallet and headed for the exit. As Charlie started to follow him, Justina called out, 'Hey guys! Where are you going?'

'She will not permit us to go down into the tunnel,' replied Rocco. 'Didn't you hear her?'

'Sure. But what I heard was the opening bid of her negotiating strategy. She's waiting for you to come back with a higher offer, dumb ass!'

'You think so?'

'A hundred Euros,' Justina said to the woman.

The shaking of the shopkeeper's head was less manic this time.

'Two hundred if you could turn a blind eye to any chiselling noises,' added Rocco, extracting his wallet again.

The head-shaking continued, though it seemed to Rocco and Justina to be reducing in vigour.

'Two-fifty if you close the shop and leave us alone,' said Justina, picking out some notes from her wallet and counting them out along with some of Rocco's.

The old woman looked at the money on offer. It was more than she would have expected to take in a typical day, and she was about to close for the night anyway.

'*Plus*,' she said, making a sign with her hand to indicate that a higher number was needed. Justina produced enough cash to double the offer. The shopkeeper stared at the money as if in a trance. Then, without a word, she walked to the door and closed it from within, and turned a sign from '*Ouvert*' to '*Fermé*'. Returning to Rocco and Justina, she took the money.

'You must not say anything to anyone about this,' she whispered. 'You must not touch my stock. If you are injured in the tunnel I have no liability. This is your own risk. I will say that you broke in. I will go home and have nothing to do with it. Keep the door closed and don't get dust on the books. You must be gone before I open tomorrow. Understand?'

Rocco nodded. The old woman locked the till and walked out.

'Charlie?' asked Rocco. 'Would you mind collecting the chisels, ropes and flashlights from the van?'

Charlie exited the shop and waddled across the car park. His VW camper van was not strictly allowed in the village. As the mystery of Rennes-le-Château had become more famous in the last decade, parking restrictions had been put in place during the summer months to prevent camper vans from clogging up the narrow streets and taking more than their fair share of the limited parking spaces. But Charlie had a particular attitude towards rules: they applied to other people. It was an approach that he always found to work in his favour.

The van was his home but also his mobile archaeology unit. Not that he ever played by the rules when doing archaeology, either, finding it more efficient to take artefacts from museums rather than bothering to dig them out of the ground. But he did carry certain tools just in case there was ever the need to indulge in a bit of manual labour. He had shovels, trowels, a metal detector, torches, ropes and sample bags. He opened the door and noted that there was a sample bag on the floor containing Rocco's contaminated clothes. He took it to the nearest public bin before returning for the items Rocco requested.

Back in the souvenir shop Rocco and Justina had already removed the glass cover over the hole and were peering down into the narrow abyss. Previous explorers had drilled metal rings into the rock at the top of the tunnel, so attaching the safety rope was unchallenging. It dangled securely, dropping all the way down to a point where it disappeared behind a bend. There was no question of sending Charlie down there: he wouldn't get more than his legs into that space. Rocco took it upon himself to tie a second rope around his chest and anchor it to Charlie's waist. Charlie would feed the line out as Rocco descended, taking his weight with the first rope. Justina kept watch for any sign of Winnifred. In a village as small as this, it would not be possible to avoid contact for long.

'How close does this tunnel get to the crypt?' asked Justina.

'From the satellite scans it seems to be almost touching. The tunnel appears to be an L-shape: straight down and then straight along, right up to the crypt. The remaining gap is so thin, they were so unfortunate not to find it. Just a little more digging and they would have broken through.'

'Sucksville,' said Charlie. 'Go finish their job and we can be out of here before the restaurants close.'

Rocco lowered himself into the hole. The space was so tight that his shoulders scraped against the sides. When he breathed in, he sucked in dust from the jagged wall. It would have been impossible to dig such a tight tunnel by hand. He deduced that tiny quantities of explosives would have been the most effective method of blasting down a few centimetres at a time. Sadly the days when dynamite was readily available in the village store were long over.

When the lights of the souvenir shop had shrunk to a small disk above him he felt his feet make contact with the ground. He looked down. The tunnel turned horizontal from here, and almost provided him the space to stand despite being nowhere near as generously proportioned as the passage from the chateau to the other church crypt. He walked along the rocky floor for just a few seconds before reaching the end. But knowing that he was no more than twenty centimetres from breaking through into a historic, lost crypt did not fill him with awe or excitement. He sighed and dropped his tools. It would be a waste of time.

The crypt, he knew instantly, would be empty. For the tunnel did not end with virgin rock face: it ended with a wall of bricks. He took a snap of the wall on his phone and returned to the vertical section of the tunnel. With Charlie's help he hauled himself up, back into the shop.

'We're too late,' Rocco announced. 'This tunnel ends with a brick wall. That means someone broke through into the crypt decades ago. And that means that the crypt has already been plundered.'

'Shit,' said Justina.

'Bumsville,' said Charlie.

'Shall we break through anyway, since we're so close and you've already paid off that old woman?' Justina asked. 'There might be something in there that they didn't think was valuable.'

'Get me a sledge hammer, Charlie,' said Rocco. 'Let's make it quick.'

Charlie returned to the camper van again. As he rummaged in his tool bag for the heaviest hammer he could find, a voice spoke to him from one of the front seats.

'Sit down, Charlie.'

He looked up. Winnifred was sat in the van's passenger seat and held in her hand the Templar sword that he had pilfered earlier in the day.

'Hey,' said Charlie. 'How's it going?'

'We're going to have a little talk, just you and me,' she told him.

'Awesome,' he replied. 'Talk about what?'

'You see, I don't appreciate what you did to me back in the church. That thing with the sword. I found it humiliating. You know what I mean?'

'Sorry?' suggested Charlie, not really sure what she wanted from him.

'Why would you do something like that to me?'

'Er, because you were threatening to stab me with your knife?'

'You judged me because of how I look and how I speak. That's called prejudice, and that's a bad thing. You assumed I was a bad person just because I held out a knife and maybe threatened to kill you. Story of my life. People always say I'm a bad person. I'm not, though. I'm a person. You're a person. We're people. Understand?'

'Yes,' said Charlie, shaking his head.

'OK, so maybe I've killed a few people now and then. Who hasn't? Does that make me a bad person? Hell no. I'm a person who has done some bad things, that's all.'

'Donut?' asked Charlie, helping himself to sustenance.

'Huh? I gotta watch my figure at my time of life. So, Charlie, I want you to know that I forgive you. You humiliated me, but I will let it go. But you owe me, OK? You need to do something for me to make it right. Because I'm a fair person and you need to restore the balance of justice between us.'

'Right,' said Charlie. 'Can I get you a coffee perhaps?'

'A little more than that, actually. You're going to do exactly as I say. No more, no less. And I know you'll do it because you're a fair person. I also know you'll do it because if you don't then the next encounter with my knife will be so fast that you won't know what's hit you. So you're not going to tell Justina or that German guy anything about this chat. I will never be far away. I will be watching you. And this is what you are going to do for me.'

Charlie munched quietly while she delivered her instructions to him.

***

Ratty was shivering with cold. Ruby was boiling with fury. The Patient was chilled to the bone and Scabies maintained his body temperature by smoking roll-ups. They all had soggy backsides from waves that splashed over the tubes of the inflatable tender upon which they were precariously seated. They were also lost. Fuel in the noisy little outboard motor was low. If they didn't find somewhere to beach this boat soon they would end up having to use the oars, and no one was in the mood for that kind of effort.

'We should have stayed on the luxury yacht,' complained Ruby. 'The helicopter has gone.'

'We would have needed something we did not possess at that time in order to have remained on that vessel,' replied the Patient.

'Guns?' asked Scabies.

'Gin?' asked Ratty.

'Hindsight,' replied the Patient, steering the tender into the calmer waters of Portsmouth Harbour. 'Lacking that, we made the right call.'

'Mmm,' grumbled Ruby in clear disagreement. 'Let's just get ashore before we all get hypothermia, find a place that will serve us hot drinks, and only then, when we've all got clear heads for thinking, will we decide where we go from here.'

'I concur most heartily,' said Ratty.

'I believe I know of the perfect location for hot refreshments,' said the Patient, turning the dinghy towards the commercial docks.

'Watch out for those enormous ferries,' said Ruby, looking up at a vast ship tied to the dock, effortlessly ingesting cars and lorries in preparation for its next cross-channel voyage. 'We've got no lights. If they start to move they'll never see us in the dark.'

The tender bumped against the side of the ferry and the Patient navigated towards the rear of the vessel where the loading was taking place.

'We shouldn't be here,' said Scabies. 'The whole port is a secure area.'

'That is true,' whispered the Patient, cutting the engine as they drifted closer to the car ramp. 'Everyone boarding this ship has already had their passports and travel documents checked. If we can get ashore here without attracting attention we may be able to board this ship as foot passengers.'

'Like hitch hiking on a ferry?' asked Ratty.

'Yes, but without the knowledge of the captain, obviously. See the concrete piles supporting the dock?' the Patient asked, pointing ahead at the dark vertical shapes protruding from the water behind the ship. 'I will row silently to them. We will climb up and walk onto the ship. We will do so with confidence and serenity. Agreed?'

No one agreed, but in the absence of competing ideas no one had the motivation to disagree. A steel ladder, slimy and encrusted with barnacles on its lower rungs, led the way from the water up to the dock. They climbed up and walked calmly towards the ferry alongside the line of cars headed in the same direction.

A woman in a high-visibility jacket spotted them first. 'Excuse me!' she shouted, halting the cars and running over to the four pedestrians. 'You should be over that side. See those steps?' She pointed at a mobile staircase that led high up to the side of the ship. A sign above the stairs said 'Foot Passengers'.

'I must apologise most sincerely for our inconvenient befuddlement,' said Ratty, striding past the frustrated car drivers towards the stairs. Scabies, Ruby and the Patient followed without a word and the woman in the yellow jacket thought no more of it as she instructed the car drivers to resume loading.

'We should all keep a low profile throughout the crossing,' whispered Ruby as they climbed the stairs to the accommodation deck. 'Don't go around reminding people you're a rock star, Rat. The Patient – don't get into convoluted philosophical arguments with the cleaners or the caterers. Ratty – just stick close to me and keep your mouth shut. We've got until six tomorrow morning to work out how we're going to get into France without documentation.'

'Wake me up with a cup of tea at five-thirty, if it's not too much trouble,' said Ratty, settling into the first reclining seat he found on board. 'Good luck with the planning and wotnot.'

***

'What made you want to solve the Saunière mystery?' asked Rocco, trying to pass the time during Charlie's surprisingly lengthy absence.

'It's who I am,' Justina replied.

'You're someone who feels the need to investigate and explore and discover?'

'No, I mean I've traced my family tree back to France in the 1890s. I have a close family connection with this village. That's why I wanted to come here.'

'Really? Are you related to one of the local families from back then?'

'Definitely,' she replied, with a glint in her eye.

'No!' exclaimed Rocco, decoding the look in an instant.

'Yes.'

'Shit!'

'Precisely.'

He pondered the significance of this revelation before saying, 'So you're not hunting for treasure, are you? You're looking for your inheritance!'

The door burst open and Charlie squeezed in dragging his sledge hammer behind him.

'Let's do this!' said Rocco, positioning himself back over the hole. 'When I get down and give you the signal, lower the hammer on a rope, Charlie. Don't drop it.'

'Don't you want to know what took me so long?'

'Not really, Charlie,' Rocco replied. 'Maybe later. I want to see in that crypt and then get out of here.'

'You too, Justina? Not interested?'

She shook her head.

Charlie shrugged and got to work, lowering first Rocco and then the mighty tool that would easily destroy the bricks in the tunnel. It took only ten impacts against the wall before Rocco announced the creation of a hole into which he could put his camera phone.

'Pull me up and we can look at the footage on the phone,' he instructed. 'It's too dusty down here.'

Rocco climbed out once again, his shoulders now starting to feel sore from the repeated scrapes and bumps against the rocky sides of the hole.

He held out his phone and the others huddled close to view the video file of the most ancient crypt in the village.

'Oh,' said Rocco.

'Shit,' said Justina.

'You guys should ask for a refund,' said Charlie.

Sunday 12th May 2013

Ratty had been woken at 5 a.m. by the ship's distorted, multilingual pronouncements that breakfast was being served. He had staggered blearily to the restaurant where he was dismayed to discover that not only was there no *maître d'* to impress with his aristocratic title – which would both have negated the need to book in advance and guaranteed the best table – but also that it was a self-service ordeal with a queue that snaked right along the corridor. He therefore found himself sunk to new and unfamiliar culinary depths; he was standing in front of a drinks machine attempting to instruct it to make him a drinkable cup of tea.

His first effort resulted in a puddle of warm, grey water in a foam cup. It certainly wasn't part of the tea family. It didn't even appear to be a distant cousin of a proper morning brew. He inserted another coin and tried again, pressing different buttons on the mysteriously uncooperative device. A cup dropped down and fell on its side before clear hot water splashed all over it and onto the floor.

'What happened to you, mate?' asked Scabies, coming up behind him nibbling a cheese-filled croissant. 'We've been looking for you.'

'The concept of tea doesn't appear to have reached the nautical community,' Ratty moaned.

'They'll make you one in the kitchens. Come with me.' Scabies led the way through a door marked 'Staff

Only'. The decor changed instantly. Gone were the carpets and wood trimmings and comfortable seats dotted around. This was the utilitarian part of the ship: hard-wearing and easy to clean. Scabies opened a second door and ushered Ratty into the kitchens.

'There you are,' said Ruby, through a mouthful of egg. She was standing against the wall, chomping her way through a plate filled with delectable-looking food. 'We've found our way out of here. The catering staff will lend us some uniforms, and we walk into France with them. No questions asked.'

'Golly,' said Ratty. 'Why would they do such a fine and noble thing?'

'They hate their employers,' Scabies answered. 'They're thinking of going on strike tomorrow. Any little thing they can do to piss off the ferry company – like letting us hitch a ride – is all right with them.'

'Why do I have a sense of déjà-vu, if you'll pardon my French?' asked Ratty. The Patient nodded. 'You feel it too?'

'It is a most peculiar universe that we inhabit,' the Patient replied. 'Connections and coincidences and causes and effects coil around each other like the strands of DNA from which we are built.'

'Well, quite,' said Ratty, wondering when he was going to get his cup of tea. 'Rather a weighty concept for such an uncivilised hour.'

'And if you are aware of the same coincidences that I have begun to notice,' continued the Patient, 'and if the universe dictates that our fate is set to continue in that line, no matter how unlikely, then our plan to exit the ship with the catering crew must fail.'

'So do you think we'll be captured and taken to the captain and forced to listen to his poetry before he throws us into the sea?' asked Ratty.

'What *are* you two on about?' chipped in Ruby.

'Patient chappy and yours truthfully have identified a disturbing chain of coincidences. It seems that our experiences of the past two days have run unnervingly parallel to a story with which we are both familiar. Either the universe is playing tricks on us or someone is manipulating our lives.'

'You're sounding as paranoid as that idiot, Rocco,' said Ruby. 'He's always convinced there's a conspiracy out to get him.'

'Then there probably is,' added Scabies. 'So what makes you think you're being manipulated?' he asked Ratty.

'Every grisly and grotesque thing. The letter from the council saying they would prefer a ribbon of steaming fresh concrete in place of my home, then it gets partly destroyed anyway; hitch hiking on a ship courtesy of the catering crew; and most damning and toe-curlingly spooky of all, I failed to obtain a satisfactory cup of tea from a machine which, let's be honest, is designed to do that and only that. It's not as if it also has to peel spuds, or direct a production of *Macbeth,* or dance the foxtrot. It is there purely to make tea. And it has failed utterly in that one task for which it was created. The mind boggles.'

'Right,' sighed Ruby. 'I think you may be straying from the point somewhat. And if all those events refer to what I think they do, then you've missed a vital element in the chain of similarities.'

'Which is what?'

'My revelation that I didn't come from Guildford after all.'

'I still don't get it,' said Scabies.

'These events are all from the plot of a radio series which became a novel and then a television series and then a film,' said Ruby. 'Ratty thinks someone is

- 73 -

manipulating his life to follow the plot of *The Hitch Hiker's Guide to the Galaxy.*'

'Yeah,' said Scabies. 'I guess he's right, now that you mention it. That would be some conspiracy! But how can someone manipulate us like that?'

'I know,' she replied. 'It's laughable, isn't it?'

'But even if it were possible,' said the Patient, 'a more pertinent question is not how, but why? Are the gods playing with us for their sport? Is it for the idle amusement of someone who has influence and money and time and nothing better to do?'

'Or,' said Ruby in her sternest tone, 'maybe it's a coincidence that carries no meaning whatsoever and we should get on with the challenges that we already face without inventing new ones.'

'Or,' continued the Patient, with utter disregard for her scepticism, 'it is a combination of external manipulation and internal coincidence. The revelation of Ruby's town of origin cannot have been influenced by an outsider and we must therefore discount it. I believe the tea machine incident is in the same category, but the letter from the council concerning the destruction of Stiperstones to build a bypass could have been from the hand of someone with an agenda. Our present need to travel without documentation is perhaps an extension of that agenda, leading us effectively to hitch hike with the strike-prone French equivalent of Dentrassi cooks. The hand of influence becomes more distant, less direct, with every passing hour, and that means the subsequent events are more explicable by coincidence than by conspiracy.'

'And that means there's nothing more to worry about?' asked Scabies.

At that moment the ship's loudspeaker system beeped and a voice crackled through the greasy speakers.

'This is your captain speaking. We will be arriving in Cherbourg in thirty minutes. It has also been brought to my attention that we may have some stowaways on board. I advise you to hand yourselves in to the nearest crew member or face the consequences.'

'See? Coincidence. And not even a very good one, because he didn't say anything about reading his poems to us,' said Ruby.

'Or his announcement was a carefully planned move that will be followed by our capture, enforced exposure to diabolical poetry and expulsion into the sea,' said Ratty.

One of the chefs approached them carrying spare sets of clothing and hats. He distributed them amongst the stowaways.

'Will you all please stop being paranoid about what's happening?' asked Ruby, stepping into a baggy pair of white trousers. 'Just get these things on and pretend to be French until we're safe.'

'I appreciate that we're in something of a how-do-you-do,' said Ratty, 'and under these exceptional circumstances I don't mind taking a yacht without the owner's permission or travelling on a ferry without a ticket, but pretend to be French? I really don't think there's any need to descend quite so far.'

'Shush, Ratty. Put your hat on and get in line with the locals, and don't open your mouth until we're ashore.'

'Oh the inhumanity,' mumbled Ratty, feeling ridiculous in an outfit that made him look like a servant.

'And if we get ashore and our next means of transport turns out *not* to be a stolen limousine driven by a two-headed ex-boyfriend of mine who has become President of France, I don't want to hear any more of this nonsense about someone manipulating our lives according to a Douglas Adams story.'

Ratty nodded, grabbed a string of onions from a vegetable box and dangled them around his neck.

***

The campsite clung to an extended night. Steep hills on either side of the valley ensured a late dawn and an early dusk. Rocco woke up to the unnerving sound of Charlie's snoring. He threw a pillow at Charlie's bunk and the tremors ceased. A gargling yawn announced the awakening of Rocco's host.

'Was I snoring, man?' asked Charlie.

'No,' Rocco replied. 'I think it was just a minor earthquake.'

'We should get up. If you stay in the van too long it gets real hotsville Idaho.' Charlie looked outside, wondering if Justina had gone. The wobbly tent that he had rapidly erected for her in the dark still stood tall, if not proud. Whether she was inside it, though, was less certain.

'Any sign of our guest?' asked Rocco.

Charlie rubbed his puffy eyes and looked more closely. The tent door was open. 'Guess she decided not to stick around,' he said.

'Or perhaps Winnifred found her? Dragged her away to her doom during the night like a bear.'

Charlie didn't respond. He knew this would not be the case, but having failed to disclose his encounter with Winnifred the previous evening, he now felt it was inappropriate to mention the subject. Her threats meant nothing to him: he was sure he could take care of himself if necessary. Besides, if Justina was no longer with them there was probably no need to say anything to Rocco.

'I wonder if she went back to Rennes in the night to take another look inside that crypt?' said Rocco.

'It's a long walk across the fields and through the woods. Only a real batshit crazy chick would do that in the dark. Or in the daylight, come to think of it.'

'But she was fascinated by the video footage that I showed her.'

'You think she couldn't wait to go back in there?'

'Well it was pretty amazing, don't you think?' Rocco pulled on a fresh set of Charlie's voluminous clothes. 'I want to go back to my rental apartment today and get my suitcase. I feel silly wearing your things.'

'You think it's safe?'

'It's not safe to sleep there, no. It's right across from the chateau, and that's too close to Winnifred, assuming that's where she's hanging out. But I can run in and out of there quickly this morning.'

Rocco stepped outside to check Justina's tent. He pulled the door open wide. As expected, it was empty.

'Hey, good morning,' said a voice behind him. Justina wore a towel around her wet hair and her clothes were patchy with moisture where she had dressed too soon after her shower. 'Thank you for letting me stay here. I was worried about Winnifred, but it looks like she hasn't come looking for us.'

'Where do we go from here?' asked Rocco. 'We can't avoid Winnifred for ever.'

'I think we have a bigger problem,' she replied. 'That poor family she murdered. Someone's going to miss them. Sooner or later the police will come to the chateau looking for them. It's the weekend, so we have a bit of a buffer before teachers notice the kids aren't in school and bosses wonder why their employees are absent, but in a few days this area is going to be crawling with police. We better make sure we find what we need to find and get the hell out of here before that happens.'

'Hey Charlie!' called Rocco. 'Did you hear that?'

Charlie stepped down from the van, gulping in the cool, fresh air of the campsite.

'I heard you say "Hey Charlie".'

'I think we have forty-eight hours to crack this mystery and get out of town. Winnifred's crimes will bring the kind of attention to Rennes that we would prefer not to be part of, if you see what I mean?'

'Huh?'

'The police, Charlie. Two days from now there will be police everywhere. We will have to be gone by then. So let's get back there right now and get started. The clock is ticking.'

Charlie tried not to show his discomfort at the idea of getting back to Rennes so soon. He needed a reason to stall things. His phone rang. The number was unfamiliar, but he answered anyway, hoping not to hear Winnifred's cold voice at the other end.

'Ruby?' he asked, in disbelief. 'Ruby Towers? No way shitsville!'

Ruby was the archaeologist of his dreams. They had met many times before, and could almost consider themselves friends, but she had never given Charlie her phone number. She was right to withhold it. His obsession with her was as unhealthy as the rest of him. She knew, and he knew, that avoiding contact was the only way to dull his propensity to stalk her. And now, knowing he was also on the hunt for Saunière's treasure with Rocco, she was calling him directly. Asking for a favour. Needing him badly. He had to sit down to deal with the shock.

***

'What did this Charlie bloke say?' asked Scabies, lighting a fresh roll-up. They were standing outside a quayside café watching the citizens of Cherbourg start their day. Ratty was inside with the Patient, seeking help in his hopeless quest for a cup of tea.

'Hard to say,' replied Ruby, wafting the smoke from her face. 'He tends to get overexcited and starts foaming at the mouth when I speak to him.'

'Are all your friends weird?' asked Scabies.

Ruby gave him one of her looks before answering, 'He's not my friend. He's more of a fan.'

'You have fans?'

'Don't sound so incredulous! You're not the only celebrity here. Anyway, I don't have fans. I have *a* fan. Him.'

'How come you knew he was here in France if you're not friends with this Charlie?'

'Well, he's friends with Rocco – and yes, Rocco is a bit weird too – and Rocco told me not long ago that he was going to France with Charlie to solve the Rennes mystery.'

'And Charlie's coming to get us, right?'

'He made some weird noises, but I think so. Said he'll be here by about midnight.'

'And he's not the President and he doesn't have two heads?' quipped Scabies.

'No,' said Ruby, 'although he does have at least two chins.'

'I reckon we've broken the curse of Douglas Adams, anyway. The captain didn't find us, and the police didn't stop us even though your Lordy mate looked like an extra from '*Allo* '*Allo!*.'

'I don't know why you went through with this crazy scheme too,' said Ruby. 'You had your passport with you all along. Why bother to smuggle yourself ashore with the chefs?'

'Guess it's more fun to be an outlaw than an in-law,' Scabies replied.

'In-law? What are you talking about?'

'Doesn't really mean anything, does it? Just thought it sounded cool. Might use that in a song, actually.'

Ratty and the Patient joined them on the pavement. The expression on the aristocrat's face suggested he had yet to satisfy his craving for a steaming Darjeeling. Ruby decided to take charge.

'OK, everyone. We have until midnight. Charlie will pick us up from this spot, and if we take turns driving through the night we can be in Rennes by tomorrow lunchtime. It's nine o'clock now, so we have fifteen hours before he arrives. I propose we find somewhere comfortable to spend the day and use those hours to plan what we intend to do when we get to Rennes.'

'This establishment doesn't even possess a teapot,' said Ratty. 'To be honest, I don't think those waiter chaps even know what an infuser ball is. I tried explaining to them that tea is one of the fundamental elements of the universe, one of the building blocks of life itself. They looked at me blankly, as if I was speaking a foreign language, but I wasn't. I was speaking pure and unadulterated English. It's incredible that one only needs to travel a short distance to encounter a land still ensconced in such primitive barbarism.'

Ruby sighed. Sometimes taking care of Ratty was like looking after a child, though deep down she suspected that his daft proclamations were made with his tongue firmly placed in his cheek.

'Problem solved,' said Scabies, looking at his phone. 'I've found an English pub round the corner. We'll wait there.'

'It will be like a corner of a foreign field that is forever serving tea,' said Ratty. 'My heartfelt wotsnames, Mr Scabies.'

***

Rocco was not pleased by Charlie's sudden decision to drive to the other end of France. The camper van gave Rocco shelter, mobility and a base for the equipment he would need. Returning to his rented apartment would expose him to the threat of Winnifred, and although Charlie was slow and generally incompetent he couldn't afford to let him disappear for most of the short time they had available.

'You have to stay here, Charlie,' said Rocco, leaning into the camper van.

'You were going to come to Rennes on your own, anyway,' said Charlie, already preparing the van for the long journey. He stuffed clothes and food into cupboards and secured anything that might roll around. 'You told me in Guyana, remember? When I saved the world.'

'I think you will find it was I who saved us, Charlie.'

'Whatever. We all played our part.'

'And now you have to play your part here. We have much to do. I didn't mind when you told me that you wanted to come on this trip with me. I am not doing this for the material rewards, Charlie, but I know that is your motivation and that is why I don't mind sharing our finds with you. But if you're on the other side of France when I find the lost treasure of Jerusalem or whatever it may be, I won't be able to split it with you. You get that, don't you?'

Charlie seemed to hesitate. Rocco had sparked an internal battle between his innate greed and his unhealthy obsession with Ruby Towers, even though the archaeologist he idolised was almost old enough to be his mother. Then there was the issue of Winnifred. This was complicated; he preferred things to be simple.

'I don't know, Rocco. I promised I'd drive to Cherbourg and bring her here.'

'Why can't they take the train?'

'I think they want to avoid public transport. They don't have passports.'

'You shouldn't need a passport for train travel.'

'But there's something else,' he admitted. 'Something about a body found at Stiperstones Manor. She said they want to keep a low profile until it gets sorted out.'

'But you'll be bringing them here just as the *gendarmes* start combing the area,' said Rocco. 'Does she realise that?'

'Er, don't know. No. Give me a few minutes, Winnifred … I mean Rocco. You're making my head hurt.'

'Why did you say Winnifred?'

'I didn't.'

'I think you did,' said Rocco. 'I understand if you're scared and you just want to get away from here. That's fine.'

'No, it's not me she—' he stopped himself.

Rocco leaned closer, puzzled by Charlie's behaviour.

'It's not you she what?'

'I meant, I don't think she wants to hurt me. She's pissed at you and even more pissed at Justina.'

'How come you know this?'

'I don't know anything. Leave me alone. I have to get Ruby and her weird friends.'

'Is there something you should be telling me, Charlie?'

'Yes,' he sighed, incapable of maintaining his defences any longer. He didn't care. He had intended to confess the night before, anyway. 'She was waiting when I went to get the sledge hammer. Told me I had to keep you and Justina out of the village for two days. If I did that, she wouldn't kill me – or you guys. But if she sees you there again in the next two days, she won't hesitate to slit your throats. That's all.'

'All? We need to be there for those two days, Charlie. We can't wait until she's gone. By then the place will be in lockdown. What were you planning to do?'

'Nothing.'

'Nothing? That's not a solution.'

'It's the one I use more than any other,' Charlie replied. 'Always served me well in the past.'

'You'd just run away and leave us to get our throats slit?'

'For a start, I'll be driving. I never run anywhere. And for a finish, you don't have to go to Rennes. You guys can stay away. You'll be safe. Maybe start again once the police have finished sniffing around. I know! Why don't you guys come with me?'

'No, Charlie. Justina's gone into the town to look for breakfast, so I don't even know where she is. I have some tunnels I need to break into. It won't take me long. I can finish my investigations before you get back. And I'll deal with Winnifred if I have to.'

Charlie nodded. The van was ready. Rocco stepped back and Charlie got in and drove off.

Less than a mile along the valley, Charlie pressed the brake pedal and came to a halt next to a stone bridge. Winnifred opened the passenger door and climbed in beside him.

'They buy it?' she asked.

'I guess,' said Charlie.

'Let's go, then.'

***

It took Rocco and Justina two hours to traverse the seven miles of ancient footpath between the Roman spa town of Rennes-les-Bains, where they had been camping, and Rennes-le-Château. Rocco preferred to walk – not that he had any choice in Charlie's absence – since it gave him the opportunity to examine some sights of interest along the way that were otherwise inaccessible to drivers. The Devil's Armchair was one such item, a throne carved from a vast boulder, for a purpose that had become lost to antiquity, and which now sat at the crest of a hill adjacent to the footpath. Justina sat briefly on the stone, enjoying the chill in her backside, wondering if the same piece of rock had once cooled the blood of her ancestor when he had trekked this route.

The final approach to Rennes-le-Château took them through the piles of tumbled stones that once formed mighty defences around the old town and up the smooth cobbles towards the castle. There was an entrance to the village here, but it ran directly in front of the chateau, so they continued along the path to the next entry point. Thus far they had remained isolated from the world, two aching travellers following a path barely touched by history. When they turned a corner they were immediately transported into the complexity and inconvenience of the modern day. Cars and vans were lined up but not moving, engines running, pollution pumping. Rocco moved closer then felt something grab his arm.

'They're cops,' whispered Justina, holding him back.

He threw himself into the bushes and watched in silence. All the vehicles were police cars. *Gendarmes* were knocking on doors, examining dustbins, talking into radios and generally dominating the place.

'Shit,' said Rocco. 'I thought we had more time. You think this is to do with the missing family?'

'It must be. Their cars are still at the chateau. They're probably looking all over it.'

'So they will have found the bodies in the crypt,' said Rocco. 'We never had the opportunity to seal it up again.'

'That's bad,' she said, 'but if Winnifred was staying in the castle they must have caught her already. She's probably in custody. Maybe our problems are over.'

'*Monsieur, Madame. Vos papiers,*' said a *gendarme,* standing behind them.

Rocco turned around slowly. The policeman wore a gun on his belt, and the way his mouth curved downwards, dragging the sides of his thin moustache with it, suggested that he was in a less than jovial mood. Rocco wasn't surprised. If the policeman had been into the crypt already he would have nothing to smile about. He might even be related to the murdered family – not an unlikely scenario in a small, rural community. But the important question was whether Winnifred had named Justina and himself to her interrogators. There was only one way to see if that was the case. He reached into his pocket and produced his wallet, inside which was his driving licence. Justina followed his actions and showed hers. There was a brief silence while the *gendarme* found their names and compared them to something written in his notebook.

Without warning he threw his book to the ground and flicked his pistol from its holster in a fast and fluid move that had clearly been rehearsed many times, his arms straightened and his legs bent at the knee. He sliced the pistol sideways back and forth through the air as he repeatedly set his aim on each prisoner in turn. Now doing the same movement with just his right hand he clicked on his radio with the other and called for backup. The crime was solved and he would be the hero.

Fellow officers arrived and handcuffed Rocco and Justina, spouting legal clichés at them so fast that even Rocco's fluent French was inadequate for him to comprehend fully what was happening. Chaotic scenes swirled around them as they were bundled to the nearest police van and thrown in the back, doors slammed securely behind them. There they found an oasis of peace and darkness, safe from the excitement and hysteria that the discovery of a mass murder in a sleepy mountain village had instigated.

***

'You did the right thing, Charlie.'

He grunted, gripping the steering wheel tightly and trying to focus on the long drive ahead.

'I don't know. It wasn't cool.'

'What was the alternative? Just let me kill you and then kill your friends? You're looking at this all wrong, kid. Your actions saved their lives.'

'Sure, but I don't get why you enjoy being so mean.'

'You should try it sometime, Charlie.'

He let her words sink in as he collected a ticket from the toll booth, waited for the green light and accelerated onto the autoroute towards Toulouse. It was Sunday and the roads were relatively clear. 'You coming all the way to Cherbourg with me, huh?'

'All the way, kid.'

'Then what?'

'Cherbourg is about as far away from Rennes as I can get without crossing any borders. So it's probably a good place to lie low until things settle.'

'Then you'll be back in Rennes?'

'Maybe. I ain't in no hurry.'

Charlie paused, gathering his courage before asking, 'And it doesn't bother you that two dudes are going to jail for something they didn't do?' asked Charlie.

'Hell no. Everyone should try it. I've been locked up for stuff I did, and sometimes for stuff I didn't do. If I don't like it I tunnel out. So it all averages out in the end. If Justina and Rocco don't like it, all they have to do is dig. That's the great thing about a life sentence: it gives you all the time in the world for digging.'

Charlie opened an energy drink. It felt like it was going to take him an eternity to drive to Cherbourg with this murderess. He needed to stay alert, and not just for the sake of his driving. Winnifred still wore her knife on her belt, albeit tucked beneath her jacket, and the distance between the two front seats was not adequate to guarantee his safety while they journeyed together. The simple act of changing gear brought his hand uncomfortably close to her knee. It was best not to think too much about his passenger.

'If I leave you in Cherbourg,' asked Charlie, having given the matter some thought, 'do you mind if I go back to Rennes immediately?'

'You? Hah!'

'What does that mean?'

'You're no threat to the treasure, kid.'

'I have almost half of an archaeology degree,' he protested.

'So what? It's not as if you're gonna fit into any of the tunnels,' she said. 'And why are you such a fat piece of shit, anyhow?'

He ignored the abuse and took a slurp of his sugary drink.

'Don't you ever think about what you're doing to yourself? Look at that drink. It's got enough calories to last a normal person a week. And what's with those donuts? You have any idea what that crap is doing to your insides? You know sugar is an addictive drug, right? Worse than heroin. The more you eat, the more you crave. It sucks.'

Charlie was used to tuning out abuse. His size made him a magnet for barbed comments, disgusted looks and well-intentioned lectures about nutrition and moderation. Sometimes the criticism hurt, but he would find solace in a mouthful of donut and the pain would quickly fade beneath the pleasant sensation of a full stomach.

The directness of Winnifred's comments penetrated deeper than anyone had previously managed, however. He wasn't sure if it was something to do with her total lack of fear or her inability to be tactful, or because she had the potential to slit his throat if he pissed her off in any way, but for the remainder of the long journey northwards he thought about his weight situation and wondered for the first time whether it was something he could really change.

MONDAY 13TH MAY 2013

The bar had been shut for two hours by the time Charlie's Volkswagen sprayed light and noise into the sleeping street. Four bodies huddled on the pavement, yawning and shivering. The van stopped and they piled in the back via the sliding door, grateful for the warmth and comfort that had been absent since closing time.

Charlie was delirious with sleep deprivation. He climbed through to the rear and squeezed into a corner, no longer caring about Winnifred, or who was going to drive, or even that he was in the presence of his paramour. Ratty was the least sleepy of the group. He had overdosed thoroughly on tea, and so volunteered to take the first shift behind the wheel. Ruby, the Patient and Scabies fell silent so fast it was as if their power switch had been turned off, and Charlie was snoring before Ratty had even put the van into gear.

'Golly, how do you do?' he asked the unfamiliar woman sitting beside him.

'Go fuck yourself,' she recommended.

'Right, gosh. Delighted to make your wotsits. Erm, are you sure you're in the correct vehicle?'

'Shut your shitty mouth and drive me to a goddamn hotel before I get in a bad mood.'

'Before?' asked Ratty. 'Goodness. One would hate to encounter you when you are experiencing a less genial disposition.'

'Are you taking the fucking piss?' she asked, her hand starting to twitch close to her waist, just above where her knife was tucked.

'Do I detect from your delectable accent that you are one of our colonial friends?'

'Just drive, dammit. There's a place on the edge of town. Drop me there before you fuck off with fatso.'

'Well, it's been a delight to meet you, albeit briefly,' said Ratty. 'Such a shame you won't be joining us in Rennes for our explorations. Are you familiar with that mystery at all?'

She gave no response.

Ratty took her indifference to imply ignorance. He happily burbled on. 'Long story short. Nineteenth century priest fellow finds something in his church, becomes a millionaire, dies in 1917. No one knows where his money came from. We intend to find out, and we have new information that no one else has.'

Winnifred turned her head rapidly towards her new companion. 'Tell me more,' she instructed, lowering her hand away from the hidden knife.

'I probably shouldn't say anything, but you're getting out soon and you seem a thoroughly decent sort, so I'm sure it won't do any harm to tell you that we found evidence that this wealthy priest chappy didn't die in 1917 after all. We know he faked his death and returned to Rennes fifteen years later, presumably to retrieve his gold. No one has ever been able to find his treasure, but we think we have what it takes now that we're armed with fresh information. It's all rather exciting, frankly. Just think, millions of pounds' worth of shiny bullion waiting for us under the ground, and no one else has the clues and proofs that we have. Anyway, is this the hotel in which you wanted to stay?'

A razor-thin smile stretched across Winnifred's face.

'Keep driving,' she said.

**

The interviews began at dawn. Rocco was exhausted. Despite six hours of sleep on the hard bunk in the police cell, he had been dreaming throughout of tunnelling. He woke up convinced that he had dug his way to freedom, and even felt the aches and pains that went with such a Herculean effort. Reality soon showered down upon him, however, and he found himself being led through a glass door into the office of the local chief of police.

This was not the sparsely furnished, plain room in which he had expected to be interrogated. There was a sofa made of leather that had worn smooth and soft. Paintings of local landscapes adorned the walls. A bookcase was stuffed with legal textbooks and, curiously, novels. The uniformed interviewer sat on the edge of the desk immediately in front of Rocco, foregoing the sumptuous swivel chair that waited behind it.

'We know it wasn't you,' said the *gendarme*, in excellent English, 'so before you get defensive and start proclaiming your innocence, don't bother.'

Rocco attempted not to look surprised or guilty or confused or any of the other multitude of emotions that swirled within him.

'Thank you,' he replied, with attempted nonchalance, wondering if this was a tactic on the part of the police to trick him into saying something stupid or even if it was part of a larger conspiracy the aim of which he had no clue.

'Of course, there is the matter of the fingerprints. We found your prints on every one of the fifteen bodies. But we know it wasn't you.'

Rocco said nothing this time. The Frenchman was getting weird.

'We also found hair fibres in the tunnel that match your DNA. But we know you're innocent. You were spotted entering the crime scene on the day of the murders, but there is a reasonable explanation for that, I am sure.'

This *gendarme* was toying with him, Rocco realised. There was no way anyone would think he was innocent with so much evidence stacked against him.

'So do you want me to tell you what happened?'

'There is no need. I know what happened.'

'So why am I here?'

'Because, Dr Strauss, you are in very, very deep shit.'

'So are you telling me that I'm not going to be charged with murder, but I'm still in deep trouble?'

'Precisely,' said the officer. 'You have violated something that is of far more significance than the fate of a local family.'

The *gendarme* looked up and signalled to someone outside his door. A man in a suit entered and helped himself to the swivel chair. Something clanged oddly as he sat down. Rocco looked on in bewilderment as the man unhooked a weighty sword from his belt and laid it flat upon the desk.

'Thank you, officer,' said the swordsman. 'I'll take it from here.'

The policeman nodded and walked out, closing the glass door behind him.

'My name is Henri. You are Dr Rocco Strauss, correct? They told me your name, but they don't seem to know much else about you. Why don't you tell me everything I need to know?'

'Can I deduce from the sword that you are not here as a representative of the *gendarmerie*?' asked Rocco.

'You can,' replied the man. 'But I am asking the questions here. Please tell me about yourself.'

Rocco's frame of mind changed in an instant. He was no longer dealing with impartial, indifferent police. This man was a Templar knight. He had read about them: the modern-day Templars were still to be found in this area, supposedly guarding something. He had no idea what that was, or how close he may inadvertently have come to finding it, or how pissed off it might have made them. He decided to stick to the publicly available facts about himself.

'I work at ESA in Germany,' he began. 'My job is to track asteroids and comets and debris in space, to identify anything that might be a hazard to our planet. I like to do my bit to save the world.'

'So why did you come to Rennes-le-Château?'

'Vacation.'

'I see,' said the knight. 'And what type of vacation leaves fingerprints on more than a dozen dead bodies?'

'A really shit one,' sighed Rocco.

***

The abrupt cessation of movement woke the Patient. Daylight glared through the windows of the van, illuminating the sorry state of its jumbled, slumbering passengers. He looked outside and deduced that they had stopped for fuel, but no one was at the pump.

Ratty slumped forward onto the steering wheel. The gentle impact woke him up again. 'Sleep,' he mumbled. 'Sleep. Need. Sleep.' He climbed through to the rear of the van, eyes barely open, and fell into a gap between Scabies and Ruby, waking them both as he did so.

The Patient nudged Charlie. 'I think we need fuel, Charlie.'

'Huh?'

'Ratty has been driving for many hours and he needs rest and the vehicle needs fuel.'

Charlie rubbed his eyes and blinked at the Patient. Then he looked at the front seats. The driver's seat was empty, but the adjacent seat contained an unwelcome passenger. Winnifred turned her head and grinned at Charlie. His first reaction was confusion. Why was she still in his camper van? Were they still in Cherbourg?

'It's fine, kid, you don't need to pretend to be pleased to see me. There's been a change of plan. I'm coming back to Rennes with you.'

'Cool,' said Charlie, sensing his vocal cords tensing. 'Are you sure that's what you want to do?'

'Sure.'

'Won't there be cops?'

'I've been dealing with cops all my life, kid. I know one or two tricks. Anyhow, are you going to put some gas in this thing or not?'

Charlie stretched and opened the sliding door. Everyone was now awake, besides Ratty. No one knew anything about Winnifred or why she was travelling with them. As he filled his tank with diesel he decided that the less they knew the better, and if she left the van for any reason during the journey he would drive off and abandon her. He went to the shop to pay and on his return Winnifred was gone. Delighted at this unexpected opportunity he started the engine and put the van into gear and had just started moving when he heard the sound of the chemical toilet flushing at the rear of the van before the tight door opened.

Winnifred emerged and grumpily squeezed past the assortment of tired bodies stretched across the bed and the seats and the floor.

'Guys, everyone, er,' began Charlie, wondering how he could explain Winnifred's presence on board, 'this lady is called Winnifred. She's a Yank, just like me, but she's not all bad.'

Scabies found the gag mildly amusing even if Winnifred didn't.

'Where are you heading, love?' asked the drummer.

'Shut the—' she began, only to find her outburst halted by Charlie's puffy hand placed across her mouth. Instinctively she reached for the knife at her side, but stopped herself. There were too many people within reach. She could easily be overpowered if they suspected anything. Charlie was right to protect her from herself. She pulled his hand away and winked at him. 'I was just going to ask you to shut the window,' she explained. 'I felt like I was going to have a sneezing fit.'

Scabies looked at the windows. They were all closed. He decided to quiz her again.

'Winnifred, where are we taking you?'

'All the way,' she replied. 'You can take me all the way.'

***

In another part of the police station, Justina was being interviewed in a more traditional manner. In a cramped and plain room, a strange man with a sword strapped to his waist had spent five minutes with her, asking lightweight questions and not seeming to care about her answers, before leaving things to the police. Justina now chatted with a policewoman who, in other circumstances, might have been a friend. They had talked about hair and fashion and celebrities and the latest movies to reach France from Hollywood and the atmosphere of joviality had left Justina occasionally forgetting the reason she was there.

'I am sorry, Justina,' said Patrice, straightening her jacket and sliding back the sides of her bobbed haircut as they fell across her cheeks, 'but my boss will kill me if I don't get down to work. He is such a pig. You know what I mean? So forgive me if I go through some boring questions. Help me by giving me useful answers, and we can get this done in no time. Are you ready?'

'Sure,' Justina replied, almost enthusiastically. 'Fire away.'

'OK. Why did you come to Rennes-le-Château?'

'Like everyone. To look for Saunière's treasure. I've read about it, I spent years researching the subject, and I narrowed down its possible locations to just a handful. I was confident I could find it, and I felt I deserved to find it.'

'And the chateau was one of those locations?'

'Yes. I knew there would be tunnelling involved, and I knew I would need to have a few hours of unrestricted access to the castle, so I hired Winnifred to help me.'

'What is her second name?'

'I don't know. She never told me. She's an ex-convict. Escaped from several US prisons by digging her way out. I thought she might be useful. Promised to split the gold with her, fifty-fifty. We planned to knock out the family in the castle for a few hours by putting sleeping pills in their food, but without telling me Winnifred used poison instead. They were all dead before I knew what she had done. By then it was too late to help those poor people, so I had to accept it and keep going, but she really scared me from then on. I didn't trust her any more. Anyhow, we carried on exploring the tunnel that links the castle with the church.

'While we were there Rocco Strauss showed up. He'd broken in to the castle in the course of his own treasure hunt. Winnifred threatened him with a knife and made him drag all the bodies into the empty crypt that we'd found. Then Winnifred disappeared, and it seems she called you guys and told you that me and Rocco were the ones who killed that family. Meanwhile she's still out there, and any moment now she could be the one to find all that gold that's hiding somewhere. And it's not fair because it's my gold.'

'Why would it be your gold if you haven't found it yet?'

'Because I'm entitled to it.'

'Right. You think you're entitled to it. That's a very unusual claim. Ignoring the fact that it's a crime in Rennes even to dig a tunnel, the laws regarding discoveries of treasure in France are very strict and are unlikely to align with your attitude towards whatever you may or may not find. So I advise you to forget that sense of entitlement. No one is entitled to Saunière's wealth, if it exists. Only a direct descendant could possibly lodge such a claim. Oh, I'm sorry, I skipped a question. May I have your second name, please?'

'It was on my driver's licence. I showed it to the police already.'

'That name was checked out. We know it's false. Who are you really?'

Justina had been longing to say it. The name filled her with pride. In this region, she was *someone*. She smiled.

'Saunière,' she said. 'My name is Justina Saunière.'

***

The man with the sword was finding it increasingly difficult to remain calm. Rocco's account of accidentally stumbling across a mass murder scene, just hours after it had taken place, was utterly unconvincing. He kept pushing for a confession that Rocco knew something about the dead family, especially about the grandfather, and the resulting expression of ignorance was infuriating.

'Why is the grandfather of interest?' Rocco asked.

'You know the one I mean?'

'Of course. I saw all their faces. It was horrific, especially the young ones. I remember the one who must have been the grandfather. There was only one old man. I took him down to the crypt and laid him to rest with as much dignity as I could manage, bearing in mind I was under duress, tired and dirty, and thinking about how I could make my escape before I became the next victim of that woman.'

'Winnifred?'

'Yes. Not Justina. She's innocent.'

'I am in a most awkward situation, Dr Strauss. The facts are that people have been killed and all the circumstantial evidence points to you as the killer. But this crime will not go to court.'

'It won't?'

'I have seen to that. A court case is a public event. We do not like publicity.'

'We?'

'My organisation. We have just lost our most senior Templar. The grandfather was the Guardian. It is fortunate that you did not find that which he has dedicated his life to protecting, but your trespass and your murderous crimes must be dealt with by us, not the police. Our authority to investigate and punish is superior to that of the French state. What happens to you is in our hands.'

'Really? You are above the government? That's a conspiracy I've not heard before.'

'Of course you have not. If anyone finds out, we always kill them.'

'But you've just told me. So I know about it.'

'Well then I guess this is not going to be your lucky day, Dr Strauss.'

A woman rapped at the glass door. The Templar appeared frustrated at the interruption, beckoning her in with his hand but making it plain from his face that she was not welcome.

'It's the other suspect,' said Patrice. 'She's just told me her full name.'

'I'm in the middle of an important interview,' protested the Templar. 'I fail to see the relevance, or the necessity, or the urgency of your visit.'

'You will, sir. Justina kept talking about claiming her birth right. Kept saying that Saunière's treasure belonged to her. Saying she was entitled to it. Then she told me her second name. She's a Saunière. Justina Saunière.'

The Templar's expression morphed in an instant. Gone were the lines of stress that pointed to his eyes like daggers. His skin relaxed, the colour returned, the eyes brightened. It was as if the sun had come out in his soul.

'Bring her to me,' he ordered.

Patrice nodded and left the room. Rocco had so far remained externally unreactive to this revelation. He didn't know if it would be in his interests to admit that he'd known she was a Saunière all along or whether to pretend it was news to him. He was in uncharted and dangerous waters, unsure which way to proceed. The Templar said nothing as they waited for Justina to arrive. He gave Rocco no hint as to how he now felt about him.

The door swung open and Justina walked in. At the Templar's invitation, she sat next to Rocco. They glanced nervously at each other.

'Can I offer you a drink? Coffee?'

Both suspects nodded. The Templar called out to Patrice, who was waiting outside, with a request for refreshments. Rocco took a deep breath and asked the question that was burning within him.

'What will happen to us now?'

'Don't be afraid. Now that we know a little more about you, we will do some background checks on your identities. We will look for evidence that your story is true and we will look for Winnifred and punish her when we find her. If all of our investigations go in your favour, what happens next is something very special. We have been waiting many decades for the arrival of a Saunière. You came here for your birth right, Justina, and if it is truly yours then you shall have all that you are entitled to.'

'It all checks out,' she confirmed. 'I have a copy of my family tree with me. I've spent years on it. You can trace my line all the way back to Emma Calvé in Paris in 1910, precisely the era when Saunière was her lover. I have birth certificates, census records, photos, news cuttings, all the evidence you need.'

'And need it we shall,' said the Templar.'

'Will you guarantee the safety of Rocco?' asked Justina. 'Obviously he's not an heir, but he took care of me and helped me to get away from Winnifred. He deserves good treatment.'

'Of course,' replied the Templar. 'While we do the necessary research into your background you may both remain with me as my guests. I hope you appreciate that, for security reasons, your movements must remain restricted until we have assembled the documentary proof that we will need, but in the meantime you will be comfortable and safe.'

***

The driving marathon ended abruptly while Charlie was behind the wheel, taking his turn once again after eight hours of unconsciousness. He stabbed at the brakes and pulled to the side of the road.

'What the fuck is wrong with you?' demanded Winnifred, woken uncomfortably by the g-force.

'Look,' said Charlie. He pointed at the flashing lights of police cars, barely visible behind the apex of the next bend. The lengthy sleep had rejuvenated him superbly. His reactions were lightning fast. 'Road block, I guess,' he announced. 'Is anyone in this van happy to be stopped at a police checkpoint? Anyone have a reason to want to avoid the cops? Winnifred?'

'Why are you singling her out?' asked Ruby.

'No reason.'

Winnifred glared at Ruby, then at Charlie, and then spoke. 'They're looking for me. There was an incident at the chateau. A poisoning. Not my fault. And anyone who says it was will—' she stopped herself. 'Understood?'

Her companions nodded, not really comprehending what she was saying.

'So what do we do about the cops?' asked Charlie.

'Turn around,' said Winnifred.

'Fuck the *cochons*,' said Scabies. 'We're almost at Rennes. Find another road.'

'I'll check the map on my phone,' said Ruby.

'The back roads are so picturesque at this time of year,' said Ratty.

'It is not likely that they are looking for us specifically,' said the Patient. 'Well, not all of us, anyway. Wisdom dictates the need for another route, but to be seen to turn around will be interpreted as a sign of a guilty conscience. Charlie, if you perform a u-turn in this van, we will be spotted and they will send a car after us.'

'We can't just sit here,' said Ruby.

'I don't propose that we do any such thing,' the Patient replied. 'Only one person must drive the van through the checkpoint. The rest of us will walk through the woods to a pre-arranged point on the other side of the road block where we will be collected and can continue our journey. The question is, who will be the driver? Who among us has the least reason to fear the *gendarmerie*?'

Everyone maintained a shameful silence.

'All right. I'll do it,' groaned Scabies, as assorted eyes began to turn towards him. 'I can't be the only one here with a passport, though.'

'I have one,' said Charlie, 'but I may have taken some things from Saunière's museum and I may have forgotten to pay for them or even to ask permission.'

'So for once I'm the clean guy,' Scabies muttered. 'Never thought I'd see the day. Pick you up at the first layby out of sight of the pigs.'

Charlie packed assorted items into bags and passed them around as they left the van leaving Rat Scabies as the sole occupant. They stood on the roadside holding two weighty bags each.

'What the fuck is this shit?' asked Winnifred, handing her bags back to Charlie.

'These are the things that we don't want the cops to find in the van,' he replied, handing the bags once more to Winnifred. 'Come on guys. Teamwork. Let's go.'

'Fuck this,' she grunted. 'Fuck you, Charlie. And fuck you, everyone else.' But she kept hold of the bags and started walking. The others followed, unsure how to react to the irate and vulgar woman who had made herself an uninvited addition to their group.

Scabies was waiting a mile up the road. By now everyone was sweating and cursing that Charlie's severe kleptomania exhibited a preference for the heaviest objects. Winnifred helped herself to one of the rear passenger seats and hid her face beneath one of Charlie's towels.

'Keeping a low profile?' asked Ruby.

'Fuck you,' came the predictable reply.

'No,' countered Ruby, fed up with Winnifred's attitude problem. 'Fuck *you*!'

'What did you say?'

'Do you have a problem with your ears as well as your manners?' Ruby taunted.

'Girls. Not cool,' said Charlie, spreading his arms between them in case a fight was about to break out. Then he leant into Ruby's ear and whispered, 'She's got a knife. Don't piss her off. She's bad news.'

'Then why the hell is she with us?' asked Ruby out loud, not caring that Winnifred could hear. She found it hard to believe that the American woman would consider using a knife in anger amongst so many people.

'I'm with you, bitch,' said Winnifred, 'because you need me. You happen to be looking at the greatest tunneller in the world. I've dug my way through every subsurface – rock, clay, sand, solid concrete. Nothing keeps me in. You guys have got clues about Saunière that you think will get you to his treasure, but you'll need an expert like me to get you to it. And when we do, I take half. You can split the rest between you how you want. Those are my terms and anyone who wants to negotiate something better for themselves is welcome to discuss the matter with the hardened steel blade at my side. And don't think I'm bluffing. You guys don't wanna end up like the stiffs in the chateau.'

'Oh Charlie, why is it that whenever you come into my life, chaos is never far behind?' sighed Ruby.

'Guess I'm just kinda special,' he replied.

Scabies pulled out into the traffic and soon turned left into the road that led up the twisting hill towards Rennes.

'Well, you know what?' asked Ruby. 'I think we should let Winnifred have one hundred per cent of the treasure. You know why? Because we won't be there to share it. Let's drop her off in the village and leave her to it. We don't need to stay here. I refuse to work at knifepoint, and I don't think any of you should either. That's not the way archaeology is done. There. I'm making a stand. Let's not be intimidated by this woman. Who's with me?'

She expected unanimity, but not against her. No one said anything or raised a hand except for Winnifred who waved her knife aggressively.

'We stick to my plan,' Winnifred declared. 'We work together. We find the gold and I let you all share half. And if you don't do anything stupid, no one gets hurt. It's the best deal you're gonna get.'

The knife won the argument. The chateau and the church teased into view high above them momentarily before disappearing as the van lurched around another hairpin bend. With only yards to go before the sign welcoming visitors to the village, Scabies veered off the road onto a dirt track. He squeezed the van onto a narrow grassy verge, more suited to a bicycle than a Volkswagen, at the edge of which was a steep slope littered with stone bricks long since tumbled from vanished ramparts and buildings. One of the wheels sank as the soft ground gave way beneath it. The van lurched towards the drop, then settled.

'Just like *The Italian Job*,' quipped Scabies, climbing down from the driver's seat on the safe side. 'You want a discreet way into the village, everyone? You got it. Follow me.'

A few feet further along the track was a sheer sandstone cliff, rising several storeys above them until it merged into the walls of the chateau with a join that was almost organic, made even more so by the creeping strands of ivy that seemed to hold it all together. At the base of the cliff was a white door made of steel.

'That's not a very subtle entrance if that's a tunnel,' said Ruby. 'I thought all the tunnels had to be kept hidden?'

'It's an old well,' replied Scabies. 'Used to be the original water source for the villagers. Now there's pumping equipment in there belonging to the water board. But let's go in and see behind the well. It's pretty cool.'

He looked on his overloaded key ring until he found the key he was looking for. The lock turned easily and he pulled open the weighty door.

'We've just travelled a thousand miles, and you open a steel door just like that?' asked Ruby.

'Takes more than a bit of steel to keep me out,' replied the drummer.

'And what else is on your key ring?' she continued. 'Don't tell me you've got the key to every door in the village?'

'It's handy to know the right people,' he replied. 'It can really open doors for you, if you know what I mean. Come on.'

He produced a flashlight and shone it around the space. They were inside a small cave, with a well in the floor, some rusty machinery behind it, and cobwebs dangling everywhere. The air was dank and displeasingly flavoursome.

'Charlie, you might have to wait here. Keep guard, but don't let the door close or you'll be locked inside.' His voice bounced off the rock with a sinister tone.

'Why me?'

'To get where we need to get, there are certain size restrictions,' Scabies answered. 'Like this.' He pointed at a vertical fissure in the rock face. Charlie immediately understood. He wasn't going anywhere.

'Not sure if I'm wearing the best togs for caving,' said Ratty, eyeing the dark portal into the heart of the hill. 'Perhaps I should keep Charles company?'

'Don't be a wuss, Ratty,' said Ruby, shoving his slender body through the tight opening in the rock without difficulty.

'I'll go behind everyone else,' said Winnifred. 'I don't trust any of you pieces of shit.'

'Well this is going to be a great team-building exercise,' sighed Ruby, following Ratty through the fissure and into a vast cavern through which an underground river lazily trickled. Stalactites hung threateningly above them and the temperature dropped so sharply that the hairs on their arms stood to attention amid a sea of goosebumps.

'I said it was cool,' whispered Scabies, his voice carrying easily through the chilly, wet subterranean atmosphere. 'We can access some of the tunnels from this cave. And if you get a dinghy you can follow this underground river for miles.'

'Am I to deduce that we are not therefore undertaking any exploration of virgin territory?' asked the Patient.

'Doesn't he have a funny accent?' chuckled Scabies.

'He is a chap of a uniquely peculiar origin,' explained Ratty. 'But despite his heritage he's a thoroughly reliable and solid sort.'

'Doesn't make a lot of sense, though,' Scabies continued. 'Just tends to witter on about shit.'

'If by "shit" you refer to the noblest philosophy, the finest arts, the most profound literature and the most elegiac music on the planet, then you are correct, for that is precisely what he witters on about,' explained Ratty in his friend's defence.

'I was merely enquiring as to the purpose of this exploration,' said the Patient. 'We have just arrived from a lengthy and difficult journey. We have nowhere to stay, no clothes or items of personal care, we possess very little money and we also have a need to avoid contact with officialdom of all kinds. My point is, therefore, that unless this cave is likely to lead us to the discovery of an item of great monetary value or huge historical significance then it would be a more valuable use of our time to address those other pressing needs which I have already outlined.'

'He's right,' said Ruby. 'We're not ready for exploring. We should sort out hotel rooms and do a bit of shopping and freshen up before jumping into the nearest hole.'

'We're not in here to find the treasure,' said Scabies. 'I've already looked here. Loads of people have. And the tunnels that lead off this river system don't lead to anything worthwhile, either, except for one. There's no treasure, but it's a cool way to get into the centre of the village without being seen on the road.'

He walked towards a man-made hole at the side of the cavern and climbed vertically using a set of rusting metal bars. At the top there was no door, just an opening in the floor of a room that resembled a stable. Bales of hay, loose straw, leather saddles, whips, horseshoes – everything, in fact, besides actual horses. Scabies climbed out and helped the Patient, Ratty and Ruby to join him, before leaving Winnifred to clamber out unaided. He opened the top half of the stable door to show everyone where they were: in front of them was the main entrance to the chateau; they were in the heart of Rennes. The cars belonging to the murdered family were parked just yards away. Police forensic teams were dusting and testing the vehicles for clues, and more police were milling around the castle door.

'Seen enough?' asked Scabies. 'Let's get back to donut boy.' He pulled the stable door towards him, but this time the hinges resisted and creaked loudly. The two nearest *gendarmes* looked up from their investigations in time to see Scabies tuck his head back inside the stable. 'Down the hole, everyone, quick!' When the others had all re-entered the slimy tunnel he pulled a bale of hay over the opening and kicked some straw around it then walked out to meet the approaching policemen.

'*Monsieur*,' began one of the officers, wondering if the person he was addressing was someone he knew. Scabies sensed the partial recognition. He was used to that look. 'What are you doing here? This is a crime scene.'

'Is it?' asked Scabies.

'Please come with us so we can ask you some questions,' said the other policeman.

'Come with you? Seriously? Don't you know who I was?'

The first policeman nudged the other.

'I know who he is,' he informed his colleague.

'Who is he?'

'He's part of that group of historians and researchers and writers that come here all the time,' he replied.

'Ahem,' coughed Scabies, 'aren't you forgetting that I'm also a rock star?'

'Yes,' said the second policeman, 'I see it now. You are a famous rock star. You're that drummer from the seventies. Hang on, I know the name. You used to be really good.'

'I like this man,' said Scabies, grinning. 'He knows me.'

'Yes,' continued the *gendarme*. 'I remember. You are Phil Collins?'

Scabies figured that was close enough. 'Right. I'm conducting new research, that's all, so can I go now?'

'Of course,' said the first policeman. 'Just keep away from the chateau and be careful. The killer may still be on the loose.'

Scabies had underestimated Winnifred. Her threats had been real; she was trouble.

'Oh I'm sure she is,' Scabies replied, and started to walk back to the main road.

'Hey, Collins!' shouted the second policeman, running after him.

'Who? Oh, right. What is it?'

'How do you know the killer is a woman?'

'Do I? Funny how you just know this stuff sometimes.'

'Sir, if you know anything about these murders you are obliged under French law to reveal that information immediately.'

Scabies thought about this and suddenly realised this presented an opportunity to be rid of Winnifred. 'Is there a reward for capturing the killer?'

'Your reward will be the glowing feeling that you get from serving justice, from serving France.'

Despite this unappealing motivation, Scabies knew he must use this chance to be rid of the rather large thorn in all of their sides. But he was open to a little negotiation first.

'Her first name is Winnifred. I don't know her second name, but I know she's the guilty party and I know where she is right now. So if you'd like to reconsider the reward situation I could put my brain to work and see if I can get you a profitable result.'

'Are you serious?' asked the *gendarme*. 'You know where we can find her?'

Scabies nodded.

'Come with me, quickly.'

'You can't hurry, love,' Scabies replied, enjoying the moment.

The policeman called his superior on the radio. After a brief chat he turned to Rat Scabies and told him, 'Phil Collins, I arrest you on a charge of obstructing the police in their duties.'

'All right, I'll tell you where she is,' he groaned.

'That's better,' said the *gendarme*. 'He said that would work.'

'The pumping station by the well, just below us. You can get to it down the old steps next to the chateau. She's down there with some friends of mine, and they are all innocent, right? Winnifred has hitched a ride with us, holding us at knifepoint.'

'I understand. Show me the way.'

The policeman signalled for his colleague to come too. They pulled handguns from their holsters, ready for the encounter, and descended the ancient stone steps from the castle courtyard to the lower level where Charlie's van was parked close to the entrance to the well. Scabies could see Charlie, Ruby, Ratty and the Patient standing next to the van, chatting and generally looking pleased with themselves until they spotted the approaching armed police.

'It's OK,' called Scabies, 'they've come to arrest Winnifred. She in the van?'

'Better than that,' said Ruby, proudly. 'She was behind us and I remembered that you said the door would lock itself if we just closed it. So we did. She's still in there.'

'The old girl seems to have taken it rather decently,' said Ratty. 'Haven't heard a peep from her since we closed her in. I thought she might make more of a to do than that.'

'Shit,' said Scabies. 'She's an expert tunneller, and you've locked her into a system of tunnels that runs for miles and ultimately has several exits in and around Rennes. Well done.'

'Gosh, awfully kind—'

'Well done as in shittily done. We just lost the chance of getting her banged up.'

'Ah, that. Yes, I can see why that might be perceived as a less than ideal outcome.'

'And now,' Scabies continued, 'she's got reason to be even more crazy at us than normal. Better watch your backs, guys.'

***

'You think it will take them much longer to verify your identity?'

Justina shrugged. They had waited four hours already. She didn't seem to mind how long it took. They were comfortable in the library of the elegant town house to which the Templar had driven them. It was located in the heart of Rennes-les-Bains, a Roman spa town that shone dimly with the faded grandeur of its more illustrious past. The desk in the room was covered with baskets of croissants, jams, a couple of baguettes and some bottled water. The door was locked and the windows appeared to be screwed down, but they had a sofa and a plush writing chair at their disposal. A long wait in this environment wouldn't be too bad. Rocco had begun to scan the bookshelves, looking for something that might help pass the time. He selected a volume about the history of the Knights Templar and sat down again.

'How long have you known about your ancestry?' he asked, thumbing through the pages without paying them any attention.

'About five years,' she replied. 'I've been planning this trip for a long time. I thought I'd worked it all out – probable tomb and crypt locations, tunnels that could be extended to get to where I wanted to go. Turns out I screwed up with my choice of assistant. I'm really pissed about that, you know. I put so much energy into convincing and controlling her. It was like breaking a wild horse. Just when I thought I'd got her tamed I realised that ultimately she was uncontrollable. Whatever force it is that drives Winnifred, you can't turn it to good. I feel like I've unleashed a monster and it's all my fault.'

'Don't blame yourself. How could you have known that an escaped convict would turn out to be a bad person?'

'That's not funny, Rocco.'

'So you have all the records you need,' he began, changing the subject, 'to prove your descent from Saunière and Emma Calvé?'

'Not a hundred per cent, no.'

'What do you mean? If you don't have proof then we're in deep shit and we should start finding a way out of here!'

'It's half documentary evidence, and half circumstantial, but the conclusion is obvious and inescapable. I can prove the Emma Calvé part, and my great-grandfather's birth occurred during the period in which she had been seeing Saunière romantically. I think that's proof enough, don't you?'

'It doesn't matter what I think, Justina. It matters what these crazy knights think. And they're going to pull your theory to pieces, which won't be hard because it's full of holes. Firstly, there's no proof that Saunière ever actually slept with Calvé. And even if he did, that does not remove the possibility that she was also seeing someone else in the same time period. So while your stated ancestry represents a possible truth, it's by no means certain or even probable. Shit. I think we're in trouble here.'

'Relax, Rocco. Even if they're not convinced, they can't rule out the possibility that I might be related to the priest, and therefore they have to treat us with the respect that such a descendant deserves, even if they won't hand over whatever it is they've got stashed away for me.'

'I don't like this. Not one bit.' He threw down the book and ran to the window to examine its fastenings more closely. 'Phillips. P3 size. Do you have such a screwdriver?'

'Let me just check in the extensive tool kit I always carry with me,' she replied. 'Oddly enough, no, I don't have one. Or anything else.'

Rocco considered whether smashing the glass and part of the wooden frame would attract unwelcome attention. The sky outside was darkening in preparation for the arrival of a storm. That could provide visual cover for an escape attempt. And the shallow river that flowed past the window, directly through the centre of the town, created a useful veil of white noise as it tumbled over rocks and tree trunks. But anyone within the building would nevertheless hear the sound of breaking glass, at least until the weather deteriorated.

'Do you think a library like this would have a hidden doorway behind some books?' he asked, nudging each bookcase in turn to test for signs of movement.

'I don't care. You're missing the bigger picture, Rocco. The Templars are guarding something. They've always been guardians of the Holy Grail, whatever the hell that really means, but now they're looking after something of great value until an heir to the Saunière fortune comes forward. What could that be?'

'What does it matter? If they don't buy your ancestry story we're doomed. We know too much. They'll make sure we won't be around to find out whatever it was they were going to give you. Let's work on a plan to save ourselves and worry about their secrets later.'

He started tapping and tugging at every surface within the room, and continued doing so as she spoke.

'No, listen to me. What's at stake is possibly the greatest secret on the planet. We're closer than anyone has ever come to uncovering it. I'm not going to quit, Rocco.'

'The shelves all seem real,' Rocco said. 'We can't break through the window just yet without attracting attention. What about the floor and the ceiling?' He stomped around in circles and lifted the corner of a rug, then stared upwards in the vain hope of finding a hatch while Justina folded her arms and waited. 'Nothing. That just leaves the door. We know they locked it. We don't know if they're guarding it on the other side. If not, maybe we can pick the lock or force the door without making too much—'

He stopped himself. There was no point in continuing. The lock turned and the door opened.

***

The rosé sloshed as the glasses chinked. Ratty looked Ruby in the eye and winked at her. The journey to Rennes had not been as he would have planned it, and the unfortunate circumstances concerning the discovery of a body at Stiperstones Manor dictated that he hadn't even had the opportunity to bring his ground penetrating radar with him, but he was delighted to have arrived and doubly so to be sharing the experience with his oldest friend.

'Where are the others dining?' she asked.

'I know not and I care even less. It's just the two of us. A treat of exquisite rarity.'

The restaurant had only just opened for the evening and they were, as yet, the sole diners. The ominous clouds dictated the choice of an indoor table rather than the leafy terrace, but the approaching rain didn't dampen their moods. Ruby slurped her wine and smiled. Provided the awful American woman kept out of their way she could regard the forthcoming experience as a holiday. There was no treasure to be found, but the village of Rennes-le-Château was awash with meaningless clues and unsolved puzzles and she was sure it would be enjoyable to play along and help Ratty's pointless quest until word arrived from England that it was safe for them to return.

The waitress brought two steaming steaks to the table.

'What's your plan, Ratty?'

'I was thinking of perhaps starting with the steak and then working my way around to the *frites* by way of the *haricots verts*.'

'Very *drôle*,' she sighed. 'But how will you start your investigations? And now that you have such a large entourage, what are you going to do with everyone?'

'A spectacularly pertinent question,' he replied.

'Well?'

'Oh, you want me to answer it today? Goodness. Hadn't really got round to assigning any of the old grey matter to the problem.'

'I thought not. But I've already thought it through for you. It's not practical for all of us to stick together all the time. We'll attract too much attention and get on each other's nerves. We should get together for breakfast and allocate areas of investigation for the day, and then meet up in the evenings and compare notes. That way we can cover more ground in the time we have available.'

'How exhilarating!'

'I thought perhaps you and the Patient could team up, Charlie can work with Rocco, and I'll partner with Scabies.'

Ratty's face fell far enough for her to fear it might droop into his steak. She'd known it would do that, and she took a guilty pleasure from her moment of gentle cruelty.

'I'm not sure those team allocations are appropriate,' said Ratty. 'I mean, in the interests of the success of the mission. The balance of skills and personalities and wotnots must be considered most scrupulously.'

The artificial straightness on Ruby's face could no longer resist the temptation to curl and bend. She erupted in a howl of laughter. 'If you could only see yourself, Ratty! Of course I'll partner with you. I was winding you up.'

'Golly, yes, most amusing,' he croaked, chewing on a piece of meat in an attempt to hide the blushing cheeks that shouted his embarrassment with such volume. 'But why would you do such a thingy?'

'Because if I don't, who else will?' Ruby replied. 'Anyway, no one's seen Rocco since we got here. He might not even be interested in this subject any more. He does tend to flit from one conspiracy theory to another. So really we need a three and a two. You and me, and then Charlie with Scabies and the Patient. How's that?'

'Infinitely superior to your prior pronouncement,' he replied. 'And where do you suggest we begin?'

'Well they've got transport, we haven't. So they should go to check out the surrounding villages and tombs and castles – anything that we can't realistically get to on foot. That means we base ourselves in the village, but it also makes us more likely to encounter Winnifred if she returns. Does that bother you?'

'Golly, no. I've had nannies more frightening than she. Her wotsname is worse than her thingy.'

'Good.'

'But I sense that Scabies wants to focus on the village, too,' said Ratty. 'He knows about the tunnel locations and who to bribe for access and he appears to have the key to every door in town.'

'So you don't want to partner with me?' she asked, pretending to be hurt.

'Goodness goshness gollyness yesness, of course I do, old wallaby.'

'Wallaby?'

'Sorry. I panicked. But the Patient and Charlie can do the vehicular excursions. I think we need Scabies with us in the village, even though the mention of his unsavoury name gives me the collywobbles.'

'His name? What, Rat?'

'You know perfectly well that which I was hitherto implicitly referencing.'

'Wow,' said Ruby, 'sometimes I think you get paid by the syllable. If I didn't know you so well, I'd be concerned that you were choking on a dictionary.'

He forced an apologetic grin in her direction.

'So now that the personnel issues are sorted let's not worry about all the treasure or the fire or the police or any of the crazy stuff for a few hours. Let's just enjoy this meal and each other's company.'

'Do you?' he asked.

Ruby said nothing, waiting for the long words that were suddenly and inexplicably absent.

'Well? Do you?'

'Do I what?'

'Enjoy my company?' He sounded like a trembling teenager making his first approach to the opposite sex.

'Why do you ask that?' she asked, downing the rest of her rosé in a single uncomfortable gulp.

'My conviction is that you are already cognisant with the answer theretofore,' he replied, unable to resist the pull towards polysyllabic nonsense caused by his nervous tension. He finished his wine too and refilled both glasses from the bottle, failing to prevent his shaking hand from spilling pink droplets on the tablecloth.

'I love it when you talk rubbish. It's what makes you special.'

'Special as in exceptional, or special as in needs?' he asked.

She smiled. He was both. But she knew where he was trying to direct the conversation, and it was a subject they had attempted to bury during recent months. He was in love with her and she wasn't in love with him and the last thing she wanted was for that inconvenient truth to affect their friendship in any way.

'You're special to me,' she told him. 'And you always will be. Do you want dessert?'

'Is that offer a euphemistic one?'

'I don't think so.'

Ratty glugged more wine into his throat and felt the barriers of social convention melt away. 'I can't help what I feel, Ruby. I have to tell you and I don't care if you think any less of me as a result. The fact is, my heart flutters and flitters and flaps like a seagull in an oil slick whenever I'm in your presence.'

'What a lovely and romantic image, Ratty.'

'Sorry. It's this ticker of mine. It's pounding so hard it feels like I've got a little Frank Bruno locked up in there, trying to get out.'

'A better image, but still a bit weird, to be honest.'

'You have an effect on me that has not been recorded in the vicinity of any other female of our species ... or any other.'

'Reassuring.'

'You have an aura of warmth and love and gorgeousness and I love to climb inside that glow and feel safe and content and connected to you.'

'Hop aboard, any time.'

'Don't mock me, Ruby. You know what I'm trying to convey, and you know how utterly challenging it is for me to deliver the appropriate words to you from my unconfident mouth.'

'So don't say it,' she told him. 'It will only stress you out. Let's just pretend that you've already said it. I will then give you a kiss on the cheek and a hug, and tell you that I appreciate it and it means a great deal to me, and that I love you too as my friend, and that our friendship is one of the most important things in my life, and that we must ensure we don't do anything silly to jeopardise that friendship.'

'Oh,' sighed Ratty.

'What is it?' she asked.

'You really hate me that much?'

Ruby laughed and walked around to Ratty's side of the table. She hugged him and kissed him, as promised.

'Is he always trying to shag you?' asked Scabies, arriving abruptly and shaking the raindrops from his hair like a dog. 'Good thing the place is empty. You'd put people off their food.'

'It's not what it looks like,' said Ratty, deciding to omit the word 'regrettably'.

'That's what they always say. Anyway, we've been looking all over for you two. Something's come up.'

'What is it?'

'Your friend Rocco,' said Scabies. 'Turns out he was arrested with another American woman. The one who brought Winnifred here. Word has been spreading around the village that they might have done the murders in the chateau, but the police handed them over to the Templars.'

'As in the Knights?' asked Ruby. 'They don't still exist, do they?'

'Who do you think has been controlling this village and restricting archaeological progress here for the past half a century?'

'Why would they do that?'

'They're just doing what they've always done. Guarding shit. Being secretive. Wearing big swords and ensuring continuity. Of something. Dunno.'

'So Rocco is with these Templar chaps,' said Ratty. 'Is there anything we need to do? Is it really necessary to interrupt our meal? Some of the desserts at this establishment are of such culinary significance that nothing short of a cataclysm of global proportions can justify declining the third course.'

'Just stop rambling and come with us,' said Scabies. 'I've met the local Templars. If you stay in their good books they're a nice bunch, but certain things can make them turn nasty. Murdering a senior member of their group, for instance, is something they tend to frown upon.'

'Rocco wouldn't do a thing like that!' exclaimed Ruby.

'That's not what the locals are saying. Police too. He's in big shit, Ruby.'

'But what can we do?'

'Follow me. And bring a brolly. I think I know where they've taken him.'

***

'This is not champagne,' said the Templar, offering a glass first to Justina and then to Rocco. 'It is the local sparkling wine of Limoux. We call it *blanquette*. It is superior to champagne in many respects, and was produced here years before its more famous rival was introduced.'

Rocco sipped the wine slowly, permitting himself a moment of indulgence while not letting it dull his senses. He didn't know what this was leading up to, and a risky and energetic escape attempt might still be required of him.

'Thank you,' said Justina, drinking eagerly.

'We checked your records, Ms Saunière. I am pleased to tell you that we are satisfied with what we found. Congratulations. You are our honoured guest. Tonight you will rest, for tomorrow we have much to share with you.'

A look of surprise had spread across Rocco's face too fast for him to suppress it and the Templar registered his reaction calmly.

'Were you expecting a different outcome?'

'No, of course not,' Rocco replied, trying to adjust his facial muscles to something akin to nonchalance and failing completely in his efforts. 'I'm just pleased for Justina, pleased everything has worked out OK.'

'Pleased, no doubt, for yourself, perhaps?'

'Well, the alternative outcome would not have been my preference, I'm happy to admit.'

'Good. Well, I'll leave you the rest of the bottle. Someone will come by later to show you to your rooms.'

With that, the Templar left. Before Justina or Rocco could say anything, they heard the sound of the key turning in the lock once again.

'It's horseshit,' whispered Rocco. 'There's no way your ancestry would satisfy them so completely.'

'No, he said it checked out,' she protested. 'We're celebrating. He even called me Saunière.'

'Justina, be realistic. This is important. See it from their side. There are so many holes in your family tree there's no logical way that they can be sure you are who you think you are. You know it and they know it. When there is so much at stake they need absolute proof, not just probabilities. The kind of proof you can only get from DNA comparisons. To do that they would need to take samples from you and dig up Saunière's bones. Has that happened? No. Do you really think it's likely to happen? Justina, he's locked the door! Why would he do that if he thinks you're a Saunière?'

Justina nodded slowly. Her dream of acceptance and respect and vast inheritance was crumbling. She couldn't deny that the locking of the door was cause for concern.

'Do you think they lied to win our confidence and stop us trying to escape?' she asked.

'You got it. I can't think of any other reason why he would say that stuff and then not let us go. Someone may be coming here later, but not to show us to our rooms. It will be to kill us. So we have three options: break the window and jump into the river, break the door and make a run for it, or wait for them to come and finish us off.'

'One and two,' said Justina.

'The window and the door?'

'Yes. Smash the window. Get their attention by making them run outside to see if we're in the river. Then break down the door and make a run for it while they're distracted.'

'I like your tactical thinking,' said Rocco, picking up a weighty book. 'Ready?'

'Guess I'll have to be.'

He hurled the book at the centre of the largest pane in the window and winced as it exploded through the single glazing and crashed onto the rocks on the bank of the river. Then he waited until he could hear shouts and heavy footsteps echo down the corridor towards the exit to the terrace before throwing his bodyweight sideways on at the door, stressing the oak until it splintered and the lock mechanism gave way. Unsteady momentum threw him across the marble hall and he landed in a bruised heap against a mahogany side table. The front door of the house was in sight and Justina was already sprinting towards it. He picked himself up and followed her. They burst out as one into the rain-soaked street.

'Where the hell do you think you're going?'

They turned around to face their inquisitor. Winnifred stood leaning against a car with its engine running. She held her knife in one hand, an umbrella in the other. She looked bored, as if she had been waiting for them for a long time.

'She only has a knife,' grunted Rocco, 'we can outrun her.'

'No,' said Justina, walking towards Winnifred and standing beside her, sharing the shelter of the umbrella. 'I don't want to.'

A crack of thunder made the already nerve-wracked Rocco jump out of his skin. He ran a few steps away from the women before pausing and shouting back, 'Why would you side with Winnifred again?'

'It's nothing personal, Rocco. I need her,' replied Justina. 'Now I know there is something important waiting for me and I know how to get it, but I need Winnifred's help. We still go fifty-fifty, right?'

Winnifred nodded.

'What's changed?' shouted Rocco, edging still further from them.

'You made me realise. I need DNA. It's the only proof they'll accept. I need to get hold of Saunière's bones. Thanks for everything, Rocco, but we need to go our separate ways now.'

Shouts erupted from the Templar house. Rocco ran into the increasingly heavy downpour while the women screeched in the opposite direction in the car Winnifred had already stolen. In the central square of the town

Rocco spotted Charlie's van, its wipers thrashing against the torrential downpour. Behind him another car approached, sliding as it turned. Someone was driving at an inappropriate speed for the conditions, as if they were in a rush, as if they had a potentially toxic mix of adrenaline and testosterone surging through their veins. The camper van halted and the sliding door roared open ready to accept the soggy figure of Rocco. Behind him, an arm appeared through the open window of the chase car. A pistol loomed unwelcomingly through the rain, on the end of that arm.

'Dr Strauss, I heartily recommend that you consider a rapid ingress—' Ratty began.

'Get in!' shouted Ruby, pulling Rocco by the arm and whipping the door closed behind him.

Charlie hit the accelerator with the full weight of his right leg, not that it made a noticeable difference given the vehicle's limited power and fully laden state. A sound like a firecracker caused heads to turn to the rear.

'Thunder?' asked Ruby.

'The direction and brevity and tonality of the sound are more likely to indicate the discharge of small firearms,' said the Patient, 'though I am by no means an expert in this field.'

'Come on, Charlie,' called Rocco, 'can you make this thing go faster?'

'Not with you guys all slowing me down back there!' he retorted.

'Maybe if you hadn't stolen so many archaeological remains?' suggested Ruby.

The cracking noise happened again, followed immediately by a closer sound of snapping and splashing, accompanied by a foul odour. Ratty opened the door to the bathroom at the rear.

'Goodness,' he exclaimed, almost choking in air thick with bleach and sulphur. 'The gentleman's room has exploded.'

'Close the door, Ratty, and get down,' said Rocco. 'That toilet took a bullet for us!'

The blurry lights of Rennes-les-Bains now faded behind them, and the road became twisty as it followed the river higher into the valley. The constant bends made it harder for the pursuing car to line up any shots, but the occasional lightning bolts gave no one cause for complacency. In places it was difficult to tell where the waterlogged road finished and the swollen river began. Charlie strained his eyes to see through wipers that were flicking water left and right with hypnotic regularity. As he turned into each corner the headlights of the Templar car caught his mirrors and dazzled him. He blinked and willed his eyes to bore through the rain to pick out the edges of the road.

Lightning sprayed the night with colour for an instant, so close they could feel it vibrating through the roof of the van. Another turn in the road and Charlie's eyes failed him. There was no indication of where the road should be. He braked hard and sent the van skidding sideways towards the oak tree that moments ago had crashed across their path, obscuring the road completely. Charlie recovered the direction briefly, made the necessary connections in his brain to realise what had happened, and looked for options to avoid smashing into the tree.

There was only one. The river. He swerved hard left and felt his stomach surge with nauseating weightlessness as the van left the road and cascaded through bushes and rocks down to the roaring torrent. The screams of fear and abuse coming from behind him had no effect. They were all passengers of fate. None of the van's controls served any further purpose.

The initial impact with the water stalled the engine. For a second or two it seemed as if the van was stuck, lights still on, wedged against a smooth boulder.

'Charlie, turn off the lights!' shouted the Patient, recovering from the shock fast enough to realise there was more than one source of danger. Charlie did so robotically, no longer fully aware of his surroundings.

Dark water oozed into the cab, but the volume of air remaining inside created powerful buoyancy. The river backed up against the van, lifting it and turning it until it began to lurch downstream, backwards, takings its screaming occupants on a terrifying ride across unseen rocks.

The water rose incessantly inside the van. It splashed across everyone's faces each time a boulder temporarily arrested or altered the vehicle's progress. Now when they stopped it seemed to take longer for the pressure build-up of the river to lift them clear. The van was getting less buoyant by the second.

'We'll drown if we stay put!' shouted Ruby. 'Next time the van stops, we have to get out and get to the riverbank. Try to make it to the woods on the right, not to the road on the left. Those maniacs might be waiting for us.'

'I estimate that drowning is statistically more probable if we exit the vehicle under conditions such as these!' countered the Patient, raising his voice to be heard above noises that equated to being inside a washing machine. 'The run-off from the mountains of the lower Pyrenees is feeding this river. It's already far higher than usual, it's faster than usual, and it will contain hidden perils such as trees, bicycles and anything else it has swept up in its path. We must increase the vehicle's buoyancy and wait for rescue.'

'He's right,' called Rocco. 'Find any container, seal it, and put it into the low level cupboards. Tupperware, bottles, bin liners, sample bags, blow-up dolls – whatever you can find. The trapped air will keep us higher above the water line.'

'Guys!' shouted Charlie from the front while holding on tight to the steering wheel as the van rocked from side to side. 'He was kidding about the doll, OK?'

They opened lockers and grabbed anything with potential to extend their time afloat. Bottles of water were emptied into the sink, resealed and stuffed in the lowest cupboards. Bin liner balloons were tied with knots and pushed into the underseat closets. Anything capable of containing air was requisitioned for the cause.

'Pressure may cause the weaker vessels to burst,' explained the Patient, 'especially when the battle between the air and the water intensifies. When we can no longer rely on the presence of sufficient breathable air inside this vehicle, that would be an appropriate time to take our chances in the river.'

'No shit,' said Scabies, serenely attempting to light a roll-up cigarette amid the soaking chaos. 'I always fancied trying white water rafting. Quite a laugh, really. Anyone want to go again after this?'

The van rose and spun around again, this time bumping downstream nose first. The accompanying screams suggested more fun than fear. The occupants were rapidly adjusting to their situation and making the best of it. Ratty spotted lights ahead, windows and street lamps. The river had returned them to their starting point.

'I say! Look!' he called out. 'Civilisation. Well, I appreciate that's a relative term in this part of the world, but a welcome sight, nevertheless. I can see the church on the left.' He pointed. Those with access to the rain-streaked windows on the left of the van tried to spot it. 'We seem awfully close to it.'

'You're right, Ratty,' said Scabies, giving up on his unlightable cigarette. 'The churchyard is gone. Well, I mean it's right beneath us. The river's flooded it. This happened before, about twenty years ago. Loads of graves got washed away.'

The van slammed to a violent halt. The sliding door deformed inwards by several inches, the glass in its window exploded in a shower of diamonds and the passengers fell in an embarrassed pile on top of each other.

'Whoa! What was that we hit?' asked Ruby.

'I reckon it's a grave stone,' said Scabies. 'We've come to rest on someone's tomb.'

With the van wedged solidly against the headstone the water level began once more to rise, reaching above the seats for the first time. A buoyancy bag beneath the water line burst and a plastic bottle top popped open. The van settled an inch lower and the river flowed in faster.

'I think now might be a suitable moment to venture forth,' suggested Ratty.

'We're on the wrong side of the river,' said Ruby. 'The woods are too far across the water. We only have the road and the church and the start of the town centre here on left. They'll find us easily. But I don't think we have any choice. We have to take the shortest route to dry land.'

'Ruby's right,' said Scabies. 'Let's head for the church. It's the closest building and there'll be no one inside right now.'

'But, according to the literature on the subject,' said the Patient, 'the church is kept locked owing to the large number of tourists and grail hunters.'

'Better not let me get washed away out there then,' said Scabies.

'You have a key for this church?' asked Ruby.

'It's not so difficult,' he replied. 'Anyone can borrow the key if they ask the caretaker up the road. I just took the liberty of making a copy last time I was here so that I wouldn't have to bother him again.'

'The sliding door thingy is jammed,' said Ratty, 'so I propose—'

He stopped himself when he noticed everyone else had already started to climb out through the front passenger window.

'Everyone hold on to each other!' shouted Ruby. 'The current is really strong!'

Charlie was the last to leave, reluctantly bidding his mobile home goodbye like a captain abandoning his sinking ship. The window was not designed to accommodate his frame, but the driver's door opened with a little effort and he slipped out into the chilly river and grabbed the anonymous hand that reached out to him through the spray.

'Nobody piss in the river, OK?' asked Scabies, stumbling blindly over the invisible graves beneath the chest-deep water.

'Oh,' replied Ratty.

'I can feel it getting shallower!' called Ruby from the head of the line.

'I can feel it getting warmer!' quipped Scabies from behind Ratty.

Hand in hand, like a group of schoolchildren, they emerged from the flood water and collapsed on the steps leading up to the church. Scabies jangled his keys until he found the one he was looking for. The vast wooden door of the church swung open and they piled inside. Scabies secured the lock behind them.

The Patient located a cupboard containing cassocks and distributed them amongst the group.

Finally safe and dry, they let the adrenaline in their systems drain. Eyes flickered and yawns spread contagiously. Within minutes, each person had claimed a strip of stone floor or a narrow pew and passed out.

Tuesday 14th May 2013

The rains had ceased hours ago, but it was only in the morning sunlight that the extent of the devastation could be appreciated. Sides of buildings had been washed away. A mediaeval bridge had almost vanished, its jagged footings protruding like snapped bones. The river had fallen to something akin to its usual height, revealing twisted and broken cars and caravans and trees and bodies.

As in 1993, the churchyard had borne the brunt of the damage. The floodwaters had washed away a swathe of burial plots, both ancient and modern. A mangled Volkswagen camper van sat incongruously amid a patch of ground where most of the graves were still intact, but just two metres behind it the ground dropped bluntly down to the newly-expanded river. More than fifty sets of human remains had disappeared.

Scabies turned the key in the church door and peeked outside. Police and ambulance lights danced in the central square. A few stunned-looking people milled around.

'Come on,' he whispered, tightening the belt on his trousers. Like the others, he didn't plan to spend the day dressed as a choirboy. With their own clothes almost dry, everyone was now dressed normally.

'If you're venturing out in search of our *petit déjeuner*,' said Ratty, 'please could you omit the tired cliché of croissants to which those sickly-looking French types seem so addicted and see if you can persuade any local chef fellow to knock up some scrambled eggs?'

'Scrambled eggs?'

'Yes,' confirmed Ratty. 'Not overly concerned about a sausage, splendid though it would be, but the eggs are not negotiable. Scrambled, remember, not raw or in a stew or served with some unfortunate gastropod or any other act of culinary barbarism to which these local chaps are habituated.'

'I'm not getting breakfast,' said Scabies. 'I'm going to see what happened to the graveyard. Anyone want to join me?'

Everyone rushed to the door apart from Ratty, who found that his damp leather jacket squeaked when he moved. He therefore walked at a pace that maintained the kind of low noise level more befitting to his status.

'My van is still here!' exclaimed Charlie.

'It is, but half of the churchyard isn't,' said Scabies. 'Come down to the river and see.'

'That's a bit macabre, isn't it?' asked Ruby. 'There could be legs and arms and heads sticking out of the mud above the edge of the river. It'll be gruesome.'

'Remind me what your job is, Ruby?' asked Scabies without waiting for an answer. 'Oh, that's right, you dig up old graves for a living.'

'Only when they're thousands of years old,' she protested. 'And I don't do it for kicks or voyeuristic reasons. That's all you'll be doing down by the river.'

Charlie stopped to inspect his van on the way to the river bank. The vehicle itself was a total write-off, but the interior showed no indication of human entry since the night before. That meant his stolen artefacts were still inside, buried under the brown silt that now covered every surface. Insurance was something other people did, of course, so selling those artefacts represented his only way of funding a new motorhome. He had no idea how he would go about selling them when he didn't even have a place to store them, and the task of cleaning out the silt in order to find everything would make the retrieval process seem like an archaeological dig in its own right. He was tired and hungry. His donuts were ruined. The challenges ahead were daunting. He sat on the muddy grave and sobbed.

Scabies was the first to reach the newly carved riverbank. He jumped down into the space that had been occupied by dozens of graves only twenty-four hours before and examined the scene.

'It's just like the last flood twenty years ago,' he said. 'They lost a quarter of the churchyard back then. Lots of headstones, clues, evidence, history, all disappeared in the night. And now it's happened again. I thought they'd put in some flood defences. Don't think it worked, though. Ugh. Look at that!'

His reaction caused the others to lose their fear of jumping down to the riverbank. The primaeval instinct to look at something macabre was present in all of them. Their sick curiosities were not disappointed.

'A femur,' said Ruby. 'The river is to the east, and that's the direction the head would have been, so all that's left of this person is the legs.'

'Look at this one,' said Scabies. 'Spinal column sticking out of the mud. Still got some tissue around it. Somewhere downstream there'll be a half-decayed head bouncing along the rocks. Nice.'

'Could someone help me pick Ratty up?' called the Patient.

'It's perfectly OK,' said Ratty. 'Just felt the need for a little lie down. Yes, that seems to have done the trick. Think I might tootle off back to, I don't know. Somewhere. Could really do with those scrambled eggs, actually.'

'Does he do that a lot?' asked Scabies.

'Fainting?' checked Ruby.

Scabies nodded. She nodded back.

There was no way to climb up the wall of mud where they had jumped down, so Ratty walked along the edge of the graveyard looking for a point that would provide easier access to higher ground. He averted his eyes from the gruesome body parts protruding here and there, trying to focus on the ground in front of him, but he could not ignore the exposed family tomb. The eastern wall was partly destroyed, revealing a hole through which he could see a stone-built, subterranean room about the same size as Charlie's camper van. A layer of silt filled most of the space, sparing him the view of the tomb's occupants, but something strange caught his eye. At the far end of the tomb, closest to the church, he could make out another hole in the wall, but this one had not been caused by flood damage. There were chisel marks and it was precisely the size a person would need to be able to climb through it. It was the entrance to a tunnel and it led in the direction of Charlie's van and the church beyond.

'I say!' called Ratty to the others, distracting them from their freak show entertainment. 'Something rather queer is afoot. Does anyone have a torch? Preferably one that is still capable of illumination?' Heads shook. 'I think I may have stumbled upon a tunnel thingy.'

'Charlie!' shouted Rocco. 'Stop crying and make yourself useful. We need torches.'

'This church was the domain of Father Boudet, a contemporary of Saunière's,' said the Patient, attempting to bore everyone while they waited for Charlie.

'I know,' said Scabies. 'Boudet was in on the secret. Some think he was more important than Saunière in this whole thing.'

'Precisely,' agreed the Patient. 'Having read Boudet's peculiar writings, especially his work on the true Celtic language, I am convinced that in his own way, just like Saunière, he was attempting to reveal something important to the world, but in a manner that would not attract the attention of the Vatican. One priest created unusual works of literature, the other constructed strangely decorated buildings. Both wanted to convey a message that would only be understood after their deaths, and then only by someone of sufficient education and imagination. The world awaits the arrival of this intellectual giant. This true genius.'

'Charlie!' shouted Rocco, relieved to see him appear above them with a handful of muddy flashlights. 'We were just talking about you.'

'I wanna go home,' sighed Charlie. 'But I don't have a home. That van is the only thing I have, and now it's gone.'

'I know,' said Ruby. She was almost tempted to put a comforting arm over his shoulders, but she knew he would read too much into the gesture. 'Let's forget about the tunnel, everyone. We should find a way out of this town. We don't know if it's safe to hang around. The police will be here soon to cordon off the damaged areas. Why don't we grab some breakfast and make our way to somewhere larger, maybe Esperaza or Limoux?'

Charlie nodded. He wasn't in a tunnelling mood. Everyone was hungry, but he felt the pangs more acutely than most. 'Breakfast would be cool,' he said. 'And maybe get some brunch while we're there. And lunch, too.'

'Never mind that shit,' said Scabies, 'this is more important. We've found a tunnel.'

'Ah, actually, without blowing one's own—'

'Ratty found a tunnel,' corrected Scabies, taking the hint. 'Which is why he should go in first.'

'It's awfully dark in there. Not to mention unseasonably moist. If anyone else would prefer to venture forth ahead of me, I would not take offence.'

'Come on, Ratty,' said Scabies. 'It's just a tunnel. I've been down more of these things than you've had hot banquets.'

Ratty stood aside and let the drummer go ahead of him into the tomb. Scabies wiped the dirt from the end of the torch and switched it on. A weak light limped ahead of him, seemingly failing to stick to the walls. He climbed through the chiselled hole into the narrow passage and crawled in the direction of Boudet's church. The distance to the church appeared to be only about sixty feet, but with blistered palms, sore knees and few visual markers the journey felt uncomfortably long for Scabies, Ruby, the Patient and Rocco.

'So, Charles,' said Ratty, attempting conversation with the member of the group with whom he had the least in common as they waited outside the tomb, 'er, my deepest wotsnames about what happened to your Volkswagen thingy.'

'Shit happens,' said Charlie.

'Quite. That phrase has echoes, if I'm not mistaken, of the teaching of the great philosopher—'

'No,' interrupted Charlie. 'It's just shit and it's what happens. I'm going back to the van to see what I can save.'

Ratty stood alone, watching the river and almost forgetting why he was there. Occasionally he would hear a banging noise from the nearby camper van as Charlie broke open a seized-up cupboard and threw out objects that were now worthless. Ratty paid no attention to the next crashing sound from Charlie's direction, but seconds later a plume of dust blew out from the tunnel. A zig-zagging light danced through the dust until Rocco emerged, blinking and coughing and looking pale despite the filth that covered his face.

'Help!' he croaked. 'Something terrible happened! We hit a problem! Help!'

**

In nearby Rennes-le-Château, news of the partial destruction of its sister town at the hand of the previous night's storm was starting to spread around the forty or so inhabitants. Many drove straight to the disaster zone to offer their services in the clean-up. The investigation into the crime scene at the castle was already complete, and the sole *gendarme* who had been assigned to the village on a temporary basis for the reassurance of its citizens was called away to assist in the more pressing matter of finding those who had gone missing in the flood.

When Winnifred and Justina approached the village via the leafy footpath, they felt as if they had the place to themselves. The silence was eerie, yet reassuring. They had a job to do and there would be no better opportunity than this quiet morning.

'Saunière's bones were moved from the cemetery a few years ago,' said Justina. 'They had to lock the cemetery to keep the tourists out after *The Da Vinci Code* brought thousands more than they were used to. But everyone wanted to see Saunière's grave so they built a little shrine behind his old house and chucked his bones in it. Just dug him up and moved him, all done in secrecy in the middle of the night.'

'Thanks for the fucking history lesson.'

'They stuck a slab of concrete over the top of it,' Justina continued, 'so we can't go in from the top. But it's right next to a sheer drop down to the path. We can get in sideways, and there's usually no one down there.

If we tape off access to the path at both ends we won't be disturbed.'

'No shit.'

'And no one needs to get hurt, you understand?'

'You know something? You're no fun.'

They walked up to the stable yard of the chateau. Even after forensic searches of each tumbledown outbuilding, the place was still crammed with rusting farm tools and other implements as if nothing had happened there. Winnifred selected a wheelbarrow, filled it with tools, and set off towards the section of path below the grave of Saunière while Justina picked up lengths of police crime scene tape that were lying around and used them to block both ends of the footpath. The tunnelling began immediately. Part of the cliffside above them was solid rock, but a seam of soft soil and grit provided the perfect starting point for their excavations. Winnifred progressed through the hill an inch at a time, steady and calm, her curving biceps exposed to the morning sun. She paused when she was about four feet into the cliff face. The bones were now just above her, and the soil would be loose after its relatively recent disturbance during the re-interment.

Justina handed her labourer a protein shake. Not a single person had troubled them since they'd begun. They could sense victory. Winnifred downed her drink in seconds and returned to the task. She hacked at the soil above her head, higher and higher, all the way to the anticipated depth of the grave. Finally, the shovel made contact with something solid. She cleared the dirt from the underside. It was wood. They had located the new coffin into which Saunière's bones had been transferred.

She put down the shovel and replaced it with an axe. Justina waited with a bag in which to place the bones she expected would cascade down upon them at any moment. Winnifred swung the axe and smashed through the wood. She repeated the move in different places until a large piece of the underside of the coffin fell down.

'Any bones?' asked Justina.

'Not yet.'

'Let me reach inside.'

Winnifred stood aside and let Justina put her hand into the coffin. Her hand moved in a circle and made contact with nothing. 'I can't find anything. Maybe they all slid up one end when it was moved? Smash the rest of it open.'

More soil had to be cleared before the whole underside of the coffin could be revealed. Winnifred then destroyed the remainder of the coffin's base and inspected the fallen detritus.

'No bones at all?' asked Justina. 'What the hell is going on?'

'Makes sense to me. You said they moved him in secret?'

'Yes. I read all about it. The villagers were kept in the dark until after it was done. There was even some controversy because his new grave didn't point east to west like a proper Christian grave.'

'So it's obvious,' said Winnifred. 'If there was no one around to see the bones, why go to the bother of digging them up in the first place? The lazy assholes never moved him. They just pretended to. I'd have done the same.'

'So we need to get all our stuff into the locked cemetery? Shit.'

'Locked? When has that ever been a problem?' Winnifred asked, lifting a hefty pair of bolt cutters from a tool bag. 'Get some more police tape and seal off the entrance as soon as we're inside. Do you know where his original grave was?'

'Of course I do. It's next to his housekeeper, Marie, up against the wall that divides the cemetery from his garden.'

'This is going to be easy. Just soil, straight down. Piece of cake.'

Only five minutes later they were secured behind the tall iron gates of the cemetery, protected from public curiosity by the fake police cordon. They turned left behind the church and approached the wall where Saunière had first been laid to rest.

'There was a stone engraving above the spot,' said Justina. 'It was supposed to be Saunière's face but they actually did the carving based on a photo of his brother.' She walked up to the wall. 'There it is.' Beneath the relief was a thin concrete slab, marking the outline of the grave. 'The sledge hammer will sort that in no time, huh?'

'Are you trying to tell me my job? Stand back. This is going to make some noise.'

The cement shattered under the first blow. Winnifred cleared the rubble and started the downward journey while Justina kept a lookout for anyone who might be tempted to question the validity of the police tape across the gates. Winnifred revelled in the physical workout, throwing weighty shovel-loads of earth over her shoulders and gleefully stabbing the next layer of soil with the pickaxe. With almost superhuman strength she progressed through the soil until she appeared to have been swallowed whole by the grave.

'Anything?' asked Justina, peering down into the space.

'Jack shit. Not even traces of a coffin.'

'Could it be any deeper?'

'I'll go another couple of feet,' Winnifred replied. 'The bones have to be just beneath me.'

But there was nothing. Only stones, soil, grit and Winnifred's sweat.

'Impossible!' screamed Justina. 'What the fuck is going on here? Saunière can't just be invisible!'

'When does it say he died?' asked Winnifred, climbing out of the pit, panting.

'1917,' said Justina. 'January 22nd.'

'And did you hear what those English guys were saying about him?'

'Huh?'

'They think he didn't die until years later – 1917 was when he *faked* his death. They said they had evidence of it. And I think we've found our own proof. It explains why there's no bones in here or in his new tomb.'

'And you didn't think this was worth mentioning before we started?' asked Justina, incredulous.

'Maybe. It's not as if you've done any of the manual work, anyway. And we don't have any other clues as to his resting place, so don't you think we would have checked out these graves anyway?'

'But this is a disaster. If he didn't die here, he could be anywhere.'

'Yep,' Winnifred agreed. 'Anywhere but here. It's a big world out there.'

Justina sat on a nearby gravestone and put her head in her hands. She'd thought she was at the end of her quest, and now it stretched ahead of her into infinity.

'I've been through too much shit already to give up now,' she said, talking to herself. 'Start from the beginning, right? So what do we know?' she continued, ignoring Winnifred's shrugging shoulders. 'We know if we can somehow find Saunière's bones and get a DNA sample, and if that sample matches mine, then the Templars will authorise me to inherit whatever it is they are guarding. Right?' Winnifred stared across the wall at the fabulous view: hills and valleys, twisting roads, distant mountains and patchwork fields. 'So that means that they've got whatever Saunière had. And that means it isn't buried under the village any more. Right? So if we can't find the remains of Saunière, there's no point looking for his gold here. We need to infiltrate the Templars. They must have it close to them so they can keep an eye on it. And we know the location of one of their bases, in Rennes-les-Bains. Right?'

'Whatever. What do you wanna do, Justina?'

'We take the fight to them. If the Templars won't give me my inheritance, we're going to find it and we're going to take it.'

***

The last battery died. Charlie's torches had been feeble and unreliable to begin with, and now they were all useless. Ruby and Scabies felt their eyes straining to amplify light that wasn't there. The Patient had long since given up trying to see in the dark. His energy was better served in trying not to lose consciousness. The pain in his legs was at times all-embracing and at times numbing. When facing blood loss and possible internal bleeding, he knew that pain meant life, and he didn't want it to fade.

The Patient was frustrated. None of his medical knowledge could be put to use without access to his legs. The tightness of the tunnel permitted no one to get close to any part of him other than his head. There was no space for Ruby and Scabies to dig him out from their end. If the collapse extended further than his toes, it might have crushed Rocco. And if that had happened, there was no one to raise the alarm on their behalves. All their phones had been damaged beyond repair during the flooding. Without Rocco, their only hope was to find another way out. And so far neither Ruby nor Scabies had declared success in that endeavour.

'Hey, Mr Victim. You still with us?'

'It seems that today I am living up to my name for the first time,' the Patient replied, 'whichever version you prefer to use.'

'Sorry, you're Mr Patient. I keep forgetting. We made it to the crypt at the other end before the torches died,' Scabies explained. 'It's under the church, and there's a sarcophagus in the middle and some coffins all around. No gold or anything else of interest. And no way out that we can use. There are some steps, but they're sealed at the top by a slab of stone and we don't have any tools to break through.'

'Don't worry,' said Ruby, sounding very worried, 'even if Rocco didn't make it back, I know Ratty will come to our rescue when he realises we've been gone too long.'

'So long as he hasn't fainted again,' said Scabies.

'There might be many tons of rock for him to remove before he can reach me,' said the Patient, 'and we're in a space that's too tight to allow more than a few chippings to be passed back at a time. I fear the situation may be beyond him.'

'That's possible, of course,' said Ruby, 'but he's got enough sense to get professional help if he needs to. The town will be full of firemen and police and doctors today. It won't be hard to get help to dig us out of here. I just wish we'd had time for breakfast before we climbed into this stupid tunnel. I'm starving.'

'I'm sorry, Ruby,' said Scabies. 'Me too. I just can't resist the chance to explore everything in this area. The crypt was cool, and it's weird that someone connected it to a tomb out in the graveyard. Were they trying to get in or out?'

'I don't know. It doesn't matter. We've been reckless climbing into something like this right after that flood. The water has made everything round here unstable. It's just as well there isn't a huge pile of treasure in here, because if we get dug out by the local police then we won't be able to take it away with us. So in a way I'm glad there's nothing of value in there.'

'Ruby is correct,' said the Patient, pausing to grit his teeth against a wave of pain that surged up through his spine. 'We will get out of here and we will learn the lessons. We will be more cautious and controlled in our future explorations. I may not be fit enough to accompany you, but I can advise on safety procedures, protective equipment and soil surveys. I feel ashamed that I did not take the time to do these things, but such was the disruption we experienced last night that my logical faculties were compromised. It should have been obvious that the presence of Charlie's van above this tunnel represented an abnormal pressure on the structure. All night the vehicle has been compressing the soil above us, stressing the roof of the tunnel. Eventually it could take no more.'

'I know how it feels,' said Scabies. 'So I guess we just wait. Catch up on a bit of sleep, maybe?'

'It would be wise for me to declare my state of consciousness every five minutes or so, regardless of whether you are awake,' said the Patient.

'Oh, good,' lied Scabies, suppressing a yawn.

***

It had taken more than ten minutes for Charlie to accept Rocco's announcement of an emergency. The German had cried wolf many times before, and Charlie's automatic response had been one of jaded and forced amusement. But something in Rocco's tone finally convinced him that this was the real thing and with Ratty overseeing the works in a mainly managerial capacity the rescue attempt had begun.

Three exhausting hours later they still had no idea whether any of their friends were alive. Their efforts at digging down through the cemetery soil to the tunnel using the tools from the camper van had so far failed. Charlie had suggested a trench running across the likely route of the passage, but either it was deeper than they thought or it veered away from where they expected it to run.

'We can't do this shit without getting the big boys on board!' shouted Charlie. He was drenched in sweat. His shovel was dented and his hands were blistered. Out of breath and out of ideas, he was at breaking point.

'It is entirely possible that in your own incoherent and dialectically primitive manner you have impacted the pointy metal fastening on the cranium,' said Ratty.

'Rocco, you have any idea what this Victorian dude is saying?'

'I think he is trying to tell you that you have hit the nail on the head.'

'And if we are all of the same accord then I propose an approach to the *sapeurs-pompiers* chaps with immediate effect,' Ratty continued.

'I'll go,' said Rocco. 'Charlie doesn't speak French and Ratty doesn't speak any language known to this planet.' He ran through the graveyard to the nearest street and headed into town towards the flashing lights of the emergency services.

Ratty grabbed the shovel from Charlie and jumped into the trench, determined not to give up on his friends. Before anyone else arrived on the scene he had widened and deepened the trench by several inches, using muscles that he was unaware he possessed, and finally punched a hole through the roof of the tunnel into which he fell with a surprised whimper.

***

'You're France's most wanted criminal and you want to walk right into a town that's full of police?'

Winnifred looked at her partner in the adjacent car seat. 'We could drive in if you prefer? I just figured parking would be an issue today.'

'Yes … and the hundreds of cops! We should wait,' said Justina.

'No, it's the perfect chance. They're distracted by the flood clean-up. They're not looking for me today. We only have to worry about the Templars. Come on. Now we know where the Templars hang out, we can start there.'

'I guess. So we need to get across the river somewhere.'

They marched past the hotel at the northern end of the town and discovered the adjacent bridge was sealed off by police. They could see men in high visibility jackets climbing all over it, measuring cracks in the side walls and examining holes in the arch supports. They continued south to the next crossing point, a stone footbridge. Its central span was missing entirely. From there they could see the true extent of the damage to the riverside properties. Entire sides of buildings had been washed away; living rooms and bedrooms and kitchens were exposed with horrifying indignity.

'Where's the Templar house?' asked Justina.

'It should be right there.'

'Next to that heap of rubble stretching half way across the river?'

'No,' said Winnifred. 'I think it is that heap of rubble.'

'Shit. If they kept my inheritance there then it's gone for good, washed downstream and spread along miles of rocky river. And if all they had was information in there about where they kept everything, I'm still screwed. This just gets worse by the day!'

'Hey, Winnifred! That you?'

Both women turned round to find Rocco running up to them, looking like he had caught up with some old friends. He was so blatantly pleased to see Winnifred, grabbing her hand and kissing her cheek, that Justina wondered if he had a deficiently short memory.

'What the fuck, Rocco?' asked Winnifred, so shocked by his happiness that it didn't even occur to her to threaten him with her knife.

'So glad I found you!' he said, exploding with emotion. 'You must come with me to the churchyard. We found something, but we hit a snag. Hurry!'

Such was the passion in his voice that Winnifred followed him without hesitation.

'What's got into you?' whispered Justina, struggling to match their brisk pace. 'One moment you want to kill this guy, now you're his friend. I don't get it.'

'There's nothing we can do at that Templar house now that it's a pile of rubble,' Winnifred replied. 'We got no more leads. If Rocco's found something we should be the first on the scene.'

'But why would he want to share it with you? Think about that. He must have another motive.'

'I can hear you,' shouted Rocco, who was several paces ahead. 'Please don't worry. Yes, I have a motive, but it is a good one. We found a tunnel leading to a crypt beneath the church, but it has collapsed and my friends are trapped. The firemen have refused to help me because we were breaking the law and they have many innocent people they need to save first. If you can save my friends, you can keep anything from that crypt that you find. Deal?'

'Deal,' said Winnifred, without hesitation.

'Deal,' sighed Justina, already convinced they were on a trail to yet another empty subterranean chamber.

'Charlie has all the tools. The tunnel is small. We didn't think we could dig them out from inside, so we've tried to get in from above, so far without success.'

They arrived at the churchyard. The centre of operations was easy to spot, marked by the incongruous camper van perched among the graves at an even more extreme angle than before.

'The tunnel is right under the van, and we think the weight of it, combined with the waterlogged ground, caused the collapse.' Rocco continued. 'Charlie and Ratty are working on a trench right now, but they haven't located the tunnel yet.'

'*Au contraire*,' called a voice.

Rocco approached the trench and saw the upper half of Ratty inside it. 'Forgive my foul language, but I seem to have somewhat painfully mislaid my legs in the tunnel thingy beneath me. Charles has attempted to release me without success and something monstrous is tickling my legs from beneath. I fear my extraction may require a stronger hand.'

Winnifred jumped into the trench beside him and pulled him free without apparent effort. Moments later Ruby's face emerged. She climbed out, followed instantly by Scabies.

'Right, which way is the collapsed section?' shouted Winnifred.

Ruby pointed to where the Patient lay trapped, back towards the camper van.

'Mr Victim's got his legs caught,' said Scabies. 'At least now he won't run out of air. It was starting to smell like a roadie's backside in there.'

'We should measure the distance and dig up the soil right above his legs,' suggested Ruby. 'We need to make sure we don't cause another collapse onto his head.'

'Isn't it right under the van?' asked Winnifred.

'Yes, but we can't dig right under it because it will just fall further down on top of him,' explained Ruby.

'So here's what you do,' ordered Winnifred. 'The lightest person goes in the van and throws out everything that's not welded down. We reduce the weight of that thing as much as possible, and we put doors or wood or any other big shit under the wheels to spread the load. Got that?'

'Right, I'll get on to it,' said Ruby.

'No offence, honey,' said Justina, eyeing Ruby's healthy curves, 'but I reckon I'm the one who should do this.'

'So just do it,' grumbled Ruby, subconsciously squeezing her thigh.

Charlie looked the other way as his remaining muddied possessions were rudely thrown across the graveyard. He witnessed this from a considerable distance, since no one would let him near the van while the Patient was still at risk. He felt guilty. Winnifred had been so right about his weight. He couldn't go on like this. Obesity had previously affected no one but him. Now it had contributed to crushing someone. He knew it wasn't rocket science: burn more calories than those eaten. Nothing more to it. And today he hadn't eaten a thing. He jogged on the spot to accelerate his progress. Ten seconds later he had to sit down. This was going to be tough.

'Patient chappy,' called Ratty into the hole he had earlier created, 'are you still with us.'

'I hear the sound of digging above me,' he replied. 'It is very rapid and I can feel the soil vibrating.'

'That's Winnifred. She's going to dig you out.'

'It would be wise if she would slow a little before her shovel hits me—' He stopped abruptly and his breathing became laboured.

'Patient chappy? What happened? Stay with us, old fossil!'

'I think I got him,' said Winnifred, wiping the blood from her spade before anyone noticed. 'I think we need trowels now.'

The Patient was lying on the surface minutes later, attempting to examine his crushed legs and to formulate an appropriate course of treatment. But he was finding self-diagnosis impossible. He couldn't bend far enough to see the damage, he was barely conscious, and he possessed no drugs or surgical equipment. He needed to find a real doctor. And he was too weak to relay his instructions to anyone.

Shouts bounced off the walls of the church as firemen and police officers appeared, running towards the group of foreigners gathered close to the wreckage of their Volkswagen van.

'I gotta go!' announced Winnifred. 'You guys owe me. Don't forget!'

Ruby was almost tempted to thank her, but such was the conflict in her attitude towards the murderess that she said nothing as Winnifred sprinted to the river bank with Justina in tow, and disappeared around a corner, heading away from the town. Ratty remained close to his injured friend while everyone else backed steadily away from the approaching officials.

'Good morning, gentlemen,' Ratty began. 'This is the Patient chappy and he needs to see a doctor. His legs are in a frightful state, and I suspect that his medical requirements are of such urgency that even a French medic would be acceptable, given the circumstances and wotnot and what have you.'

The firemen shrugged their shoulders at Ratty and started attending to the Patient's injuries. One of them called for medical assistance on his radio. The *gendarmes* snooped around the graveyard looking at the damage while a pair of medics arrived carrying a stretcher.

'Don't worry, Patient chappy. These people may lack the level of sophistication to create a satisfactory cup of tea, but they probably have at least a modest spread of primitive medical skills. Once you're a tad less under the weather we'll get you back to Blighty and in the hands of a doctor with a real medical degree, I promise.'

The Patient showed no response. The medics checked for a pulse and inserted a drip.

'What is the patient's name?' asked one of them as they slid him onto the stretcher and picked him up.

Ratty had hoped this question would never arise. It could lead to an infinite loop and it wasn't the way he wished to spend the remainder of his days. 'It doesn't matter. Can I accompany the unfortunate fellow on his medicinal journey?'

'We have too many casualties. There's no room in the ambulances. He will be taken to the hospital at Quillan and you can look for him there.'

'Please take care of him,' said Ratty, watching them go. 'He's a thoroughly decent egg.'

He looked around for the others, but they had vanished rather than hang around in the presence of curious police officers. Ratty was suddenly and unexpectedly alone. A wave of guilt washed over him. It was his fault that the Patient had suffered those injuries. If he hadn't come on this treasure hunt the Patient would be in perfect health. He cursed his poverty and his greed and his inability to think of any means of earning money other than by digging it out of the ground.

Scabies carried a plastic tray laden with croissants down to a jumble of boulders beside the river to the south of the town. He held the tray out for hungry hands to snatch at. Rocco and Ruby grabbed two each. Charlie closed his eyes and put his hands in his pockets.

'Not hungry, Charlie?' asked Scabies, starting to munch.

'It's all my fault,' Charlie replied. 'If I wasn't such a fat piece of shit that tunnel wouldn't have collapsed.'

'Don't blame yourself, Charlie,' said Ruby, once again almost tempted to offer a comforting arm but remembering to resist her instincts.

'I'm not going to eat anything ever again.'

'I'm not sure that's a very sensible dietary plan,' said Ruby. 'You should cut your calories and replace some carbs with proteins, but you can't eat nothing. That's not realistic or healthy or sensible.'

'When have I ever been any of those things?'

'You got me there,' she conceded.

'Does anyone think it's weird that the Templars were so crazy at us last night, and today there's been no sign of them?' asked Rocco.

'Did anyone see what happened to them after we drove into the river?' asked Scabies. Everyone shook their heads. 'Right Charlie, you want to get thin, right? Walk up the road to where that tree fell, right where we drove into the water, and tell us what you find.'

Charlie sprang to his feet with unaccustomed vigour. 'I'm on it!' he shouted, marching away.

'I'm trying not to think about those thighs chafing,' said Scabies. 'He's probably run out of talcum powder.'

'Should we save him a croissant?' asked Ruby. 'He'll have earned it.'

'No,' said Rocco, helping himself to the last one. 'His reserves will last a bit longer.'

Minutes later Charlie returned. His skin glowed with apparent delight at the unfamiliar burst of exercise. 'They hit the tree,' he said. 'If that's their car, they hit the fallen tree hard. The car is smashed completely. No one inside, but part of the roof has been cut off and there's blood everywhere. It's pretty cool, actually.'

'So those Templars are either dead or in hospital,' said Rocco. 'And that is very helpful for us.'

'We should search the car,' announced Scabies. 'Let's check it over before they tow it away and clear the road.'

'You won't find anything,' said Charlie.

'How do you know?' asked Ruby. 'Honestly, I sometimes find your defeatism so depressing, Charlie. You'll never get anywhere in life unless you change your attitude. Be positive, Charlie. Don't assume you know something without doing the work.'

Charlie reached inside his pocket. 'I know because I already did the work,' he told them, beaming with pride at his ingenuity. 'I searched the car while I was there, and this was in the trunk.'

He produced a set of keys. Scabies snatched them from his hand and looked at them closely. 'Could be for anything,' he said. 'There's nothing written on them. Probably just the keys to their gaff.'

'Just what I thought,' said Charlie. 'But then I carried on searching the car. Glove compartment, door pockets, under the seats, behind the sun visors. And I found this.' He reached into a pocket and pulled out a bundle of papers.

'Pass them round,' said Ruby. 'Let's all look at that stuff.'

Charlie gave her a folded document. An insurance certificate for the car, made out to an organisation, not an individual. 'ATDF' was the name of the insured party and the address was a property in Rennes-les-Bains.

'Means nothing to me,' said Ruby.

Rocco leaned across and examined it. 'That address could be the house that was washed away by the flood,' he said. 'I heard the American women talking about it. Just a pile of rubble now.'

More documents were circulated. Scabies looked at a small piece of paper: a pay and display parking receipt from Limoux, dated two months ago. 'So we know the Templars buy their bog rolls in Limoux,' he said. 'What have you got, Rocco?'

'It is a notebook. It has all sorts of handwriting.' He scanned its contents, looking for anything of significance. One page stood out, virtually screaming for his attention. 'Oh my goodness!' shouted Rocco. 'This is not possible!'

'What does it say?' asked Ruby.

'I have not been there, but I am familiar with this address. And, of course, the name … Look.' He passed the notebook to her, open at the page that he'd found so alarming.

'Lord Ballashiels,' she read, 'Stiperstones Manor, Shropshire, Angleterre.'

'Hey, I know that place,' said Charlie. 'It's the Hamster dude!'

'Talking of which, where did he go?' asked Ruby, suddenly aware of Ratty's absence. She felt guilty for losing him. He wasn't best suited to being unaccompanied.

'Maybe he stuck with the Patient,' said Rocco.

'Question is,' said Scabies, 'how did Ratty get on the radar of these guys? It doesn't make any sense. He's only been in the Saunière treasure-hunting game for a few days. That notebook doesn't look new, and there are loads of pages of stuff written after he gets a mention.'

'You mean Ratty was being targeted by the Templars before it even occurred to him to investigate Saunière's imaginary gold?' asked Ruby. 'That's impossible. It makes no sense at all.'

'Welcome to the world of Bérenger Saunière,' said Scabies. 'Nothing makes sense here. Don't worry. You get used to it.'

'These temple dudes,' said Charlie.

'Templar,' corrected Ruby, flicking through the notebook and reading the handwritten passages and phrases as she spoke.

'Whatever. These guys are a secret society, right?'

'I think *secretive* is a more appropriate description,' Ruby added, without looking up from the book. 'People know they exist. They just like to keep themselves to themselves.'

'What I mean—' Charlie attempted to continue before Ruby cut him off yet again.

'Of course, the term *secretive* should really apply to all so-called secret societies, not just the Templars.'

Charlie took a deep breath. Words were about to exit his mouth that he'd never thought he would say. Whether it was the lack of sleep, or the brush with death, or his inability to cope with the guilt at what he had done to the Patient, he had no idea, but when the words started to flow he couldn't turn off the tap.

'You know what I feel about you Ruby. You know I'm your biggest fan, and maybe that's true in more ways than it should be, and you've no idea how many nights I've spent fantasising about you and me dating, living together, married, whatever, all that shit. Well, no more, Ruby. Because I've just learned something. I know I'm not a fast learner and that's why it took me a couple of years to get it, but I've realised what a pain in the ass you really are. I don't want to marry you, or live with you, or even take you to dinner. There. It's said. I won't obsess over you any more. Go find yourself another fan, if you've got any others. Which I doubt.'

Charlie felt sick. He knew he had no realistic chance of ever becoming Ruby's other half, so he'd had nothing to lose, but it hurt him to have said such things about someone he usually cared deeply about. And now the damage was done. He would have to be a man and deal with it.

'I'm sorry, Charlie,' said Ruby, closing the notebook.

'Well I am too, but it's cool that you said it. Anyhow, I've said what I've said, and we should move forward now.'

'I meant "sorry, could you say all that again"? I was reading something interesting in this book.'

'Huh?'

'Never mind. Look at this page. Right after it mentions Ratty and his address.' She showed him the text she had just read, knowing that he wouldn't have a clue what it meant.

'It's written in Chinese,' said Charlie. 'I don't speak Chinese.'

Ruby shook her head in disbelief. She showed it to Rocco and Scabies.

'Charlie's close,' said Rocco. 'It's not French. Not Chinese, either. It's a Latin text.'

'*Absens haeres non erit*,' said Ruby. 'Those absent will not inherit, or something like that – Latin is not my strongest subject area. But look at the other notes around it. It's like someone was putting together the rough draft of a letter. Something to do with inheritance rights.'

'Justina thinks she's going to inherit whatever Saunière left behind,' said Rocco. 'The Templars said they'd just give it to her if her lineage could be proved. Which, I must add, it cannot. I don't see how anyone can demonstrate beyond doubt that they stem from an illicit affair between a priest and a singer more than a century ago unless they have access to the DNA samples they need.'

'Does it say who the letter will be addressed to?' asked Scabies. 'You said it had Ratty's address in it. Was it sent to him?'

'No,' she replied. 'It looks like there's a local address tucked in there. A street in Quillan. Probably a solicitor.'

'Let me see,' said Scabies. 'I don't understand all these scribbles, but I don't think it's meant to be a letter to a legal geezer. Some of the passages are in French. Look, it mentions '*détruirez la maison*'. Even a drummer can see that means knock the fucking house down. This isn't the draft of a legal letter. It's the draft of an *illegal* letter. These guys were hiring someone to do their dirty work.'

'To knock Stiperstones Manor down?' asked Ruby. 'Why on earth would they want to do something like that to someone they know nothing about?'

'Didn't you say Ratty got a letter from the council saying they were going to flatten his gaff?' asked Scabies. Ruby nodded. 'Did anyone bother to check with the council if that letter was real?'

'The fire brigade seemed to know about it,' she answered.

'Doesn't mean shit,' he said. 'You don't know how far the influence of these guys can stretch. How hard can it be to spread a rumour about a bypass throughout a small community?'

'Ratty said he felt like someone was manipulating his life from afar,' said Ruby. 'If we can find out who the Templars hired to do this, maybe we can find out why?'

'So we need to go to that address in Quillan,' said Scabies. 'It's a long walk. Shame Charlie's such a shit driver.'

'What about poor Ratty?' Ruby asked. 'We don't know where he is and we need to tell him the Templars have their sights on him and on his house.'

'Charlie and Rocco will go to Quillan,' said Scabies. 'You guys cool with that?'

'I speak French,' said Rocco, so it will be no problem to speak to whoever is at this address.'

'Right. I'll stay here with Ruby and look for Ratty. Everyone watch each other's backs. We don't know if the Templars are still after us. We don't know what those crazy American birds are planning. And we don't know if the *gendarmes* are likely to take a close interest in anything we get up to.'

'Let us try to meet up by the church in Rennes-le-Château tonight,' said Rocco. 'I will take you to my apartment and we can stay there. I don't think we need to fear Winnifred now that she's proved that she's capable of saving the Patient's life, and that we owe her.'

'How are you going to get to Quillan?' Ruby asked.

'My phone is broken and Charlie's camping car is broken, but my thumb is still working,' he replied, holding his hitch-hiking thumb out in demonstration. 'We are not pretty in these dirty clothes, but many people are like us today. I think someone will give us a ride.'

'Don't fancy their chances,' whispered Scabies as the two groups parted.

***

Less than a kilometre to the north of Rennes-les-Bains, Winnifred stretched out her aching body in the Roman baths adjacent to the river and hidden from public view by the road bridge above. These stone bathtubs built into alcoves in the rock had survived the flood intact, and relaxing water still flowed into them from natural hot springs, as it had done for thousands of years.

'Do you have to do this naked?' Justina asked, perched uncomfortably on the steps beside one of the baths.

'It's how it's always been done. The Romans wouldn't get their togas wet in here. Why would I want to?'

'Because your clothes are disgusting, covered in crap, soaked with sweat. Do I need to go on?'

'Chill out, Justina. Whip your stuff off and jump into one of these things. It'll do you good.'

'No,' she replied. 'Someone might come down here. And we need to think of a plan. Rocco said they found a crypt under the church here. He said we could keep half of whatever was in there. We never got a chance to go in there before the cops arrived. We should go back.'

'Have you learned nothing since we got here? If he said he'd already found it, and if he offered you half, that can only mean there's Jack shit inside it. Don't waste your time.'

'Well we can't get in the Templar house because it's not there any more. We don't have Saunière's bones and we don't know where they're guarding his gold. We're out of options. I can't think of a way forward.'

Winnifred sat up, reached out towards Justina, and yanked her backwards into the shallow bath, laughing hysterically as her associate spluttered and screamed in protest at her unexpected dunking.

'Not funny, asshole,' Justina mumbled, wriggling to get upright and climb out.

'Don't get out. Lie back. Relax your mind. Then you'll know what to do next.'

Justina stopped herself. Her brain was overloaded and stressed. Winnifred had a point. She closed her eyes and lay back, letting the warm water nourish every tired part of her body. Instantly she knew what she must do. It would look ugly. It would seem unkind. It wasn't something she felt comfortable doing and it was going to involve the biggest risk she had yet taken, but she knew it was her last chance.

'Do you know where Ratty was going to?' she asked Winnifred.

'Dunno. Probably to the hospital at Quillan to see that weird friend of his that I saved. Why?'

'You still have your knife, right?'

***

The hospital corridor smelled like a hospital corridor, and Ratty wasn't sure if he could take much more of the aroma of excessive cleanliness. It was as far removed from the homely and sometimes farmyard-like smells of Stiperstones Manor as it was possible to be. There were surfaces back home that in recent decades had not encountered a broom, let alone bleach. The Patient had yet to return from the operating theatre, and Ratty had no outlet for the boredom and frustration that he was experiencing. The magazines available were aimed at a predominately female readership, and he failed to concentrate when he flicked through pages of gossip in French about whichever celebrity he had never heard of was considering divorcing another celebrity that he didn't care about.

A doctor appeared. He approached Ratty and offered to shake his hand. 'I am Dr Wainwright. Are you here for the man with the leg injuries?'

'Yes,' said Ratty, relieved to be conversing in his mother tongue. 'Am I to infer from your name and accent that you are not indigenous to these parts?'

'Well spotted. I've lived here a few years, though.'

'Golly. So how are his Mystics?'

'Mystics?' asked the doctor.

'Mystic Megs. Legs,' explained Ratty. 'It is the common parlance in London, so I am told. Don't they teach you anything at medical school these days?'

'Cockney rhyming slang was a module I didn't take, to my lasting regret. So, his legs, as we call them in the medical profession, have multiple fractures. They required metal pins and several transfusions, but he will live and he will even be able to walk, eventually. He's been taken to ward seven on the floor below. Oh, and I need to ask you for his personal details. We have no name on record.'

'It's a long story, doctor. Suffice to say the fellow is no stranger to the medical environment, and as such he has always been known as the Patient. With a capital P.'

The doctor's face displayed dissatisfaction as he wrote this in his notes. 'Nationality?'

'British of course. Can you not tell from my demeanour?'

'The Patient's nationality,' he sighed.

'Guatemalan.'

'Ah, so he won't be covered by EU reciprocal medical treatment rules. Does he have medical insurance, or will you be paying his bill? Surgery of this nature won't be cheap.'

'His bill?'

'We had a team of three surgeons and seven support staff in theatre, and it took us four hours to put him back together. I don't have a final figure for his treatment, but I'd guess that with post-operative care and rehabilitation included, you're probably looking at about forty thousand Euros.'

'As little as that?' asked Ratty. 'Hmm, let me think. Golly, what's that outside the window?' Ratty pointed, spun round, and ran to the door at the end of the corridor. It was locked. He looked back and saw Dr

Wainwright standing with his hands on his hips, waiting for Ratty to return. 'That's better,' puffed Ratty. 'Just had an impulse for a little exercise. Spontaneity is the mother of all thingies. Or something.'

'I take it the Patient has no insurance and you are not in a position to pay for his treatment?' asked the doctor.

'Such a statement would not be entirely without factual basis,' Ratty replied, head hung low.

'It's all right, don't panic. There are discretionary funds available. We will sort something out. He's on ward seven, remember.'

'Upstairs?'

'Downstairs.' The doctor departed.

Ratty found the stairs and had descended one flight when he found himself face-to-face with Winnifred and Justina.

'Goodness gracious,' he declared. 'Have you come to visit the unfortunate fellow, too? I'm sure he would appreciate the opportunity to thank you for all the digging and rescuing and wotnot.'

'Actually, Ratty, something has come up,' said Justina. 'It's an emergency and we really need your expertise and brainpower. You can come and see the Patient another time. We have to go now.'

'Of course. But I think it would be an unforgivably poor show not to say a brief how do you do to Patient chappy first.'

'No,' insisted Justina. 'You must come with us. No detours.'

'I say. What can be so important that one can't spare five minutes for an injured chum?'

Winnifred produced her knife and held it close to Ratty's stomach. 'This,' she told him.

'Ah, well, that puts it in a somewhat clearer perspective.'

'Don't try anything stupid,' said Justina.

'That rather narrows my options,' replied Ratty. 'Doing stupid things is what I'm best at.'

'Just come with us, don't say or do anything to annoy Winnifred, and you won't get hurt. Understand?'

'Er, what if I were to irritate you, whilst maintaining a perfectly pleasant and mutually satisfying relationship with Winnifred?'

'Like you're doing right now? Just shut up and come with us. We don't have time for this shit.'

'This is all most intriguing. Where are we going? Have you found something?'

'Just tell him, Justina. It's the only way to make him stop talking.'

Justina nodded. Ratty was getting under her skin already. 'Right,' she said, checking there was no one close to them on the staircase, 'we are kidnapping you. OK?'

'Perfectly,' Ratty replied, looking almost flattered. 'And?'

'And nothing. That's it. We're taking you hostage. Your friends then have forty-eight hours to find Saunière's treasure and deliver it to me. That treasure is my rightful inheritance, don't forget.'

'I believe you may have mentioned it before.'

'So, if your friends do this for me, I will let you go. No harm will be done. I mean that. I don't want to hurt you. This is purely business, and you will be looked after very well, and when my inheritance is delivered I promise you will be free. Got that?'

'What a thoroughly ingenious plan,' said Ratty. 'I must admit to possessing a hint of admiration for your courageous thinking and a smidgen of jealousy that it hadn't occurred to me to embark on a similar pursuit. I must ask, however, if you had thought about in what manner you intend to inform my friends of this wonderful scheme? All of our phones perished in the flood last night.'

Justina looked at Winnifred blankly.

'Shit,' said Winnifred.

'Where are they?' asked Justina.

'I haven't the foggiest,' said Ratty. 'But other than that it was a sound plan. Don't despair, however. I have a suggestion that might save the day.'

'Yes?' asked Justina.

'We go to see Patient chappy in his bed. We tell him about your marvellous arrangement, and then he can relay the appropriate information to the others.'

'Does he know where they are?' asked Winnifred.

'No, but if they have shreds of decency of the type from which everyone can at times benefit, present company particularly included, I suspect this establishment will shortly be graced with their presence.'

'What the fuck?'

'It's OK, Winnifred. He's right. Sooner or later the others will come by to visit him.'

They followed Ratty to the Patient's bedside. His legs were protected from the weight of the bedsheets by a small arch. He smiled at them.

'I love this place,' he said, pointing at the large ward around him. It was crammed with beds and curtains and worried visitors and nonchalant nurses. 'The medicine, the people, the smells, the procedures. This hospital brings to life all the things about which I spent so many years reading. Isn't it wonderful? I can think of no more fascinating place to spend a few weeks.'

'Didn't I say he was weird?' whispered Winnifred, sitting herself next to the bed in the only available visitor's chair.

'They say the operation went tickety-boo,' said Ratty.

- 164 -

'Such a pity about their insistence on the need for a general anaesthetic, though,' complained the Patient. 'I was unable to have any input on the surgical decisions made, which is a pity because I have an idea for a new method of pinning the bone. It involves fewer screws by placing them further—' He stopped himself. He could tell that Ratty was starting to lose the colour in his cheeks. 'It is too late now, of course, barring further accidents.'

'Are you a doctor or something?' asked Justina.

'No,' he replied. 'Just a patient.'

'Well, Patient chappy, whilst it would be spiffing to discuss your bionic implants all day, I have to inform you of something of much importance. It turns out that I have been kidnapped.'

'Indeed?' asked the Patient, sitting up straighter and starting to fuss around with his pillow and bedsheets.

'Rather a funny story, actually. You see it turns out-'

'Listen up,' interrupted Winnifred. 'We are taking him hostage. Tell your friends, when they visit you, that they have forty-eight hours to find Justina's inheritance, Saunière's gold, whatever you want to call it, and deliver it to us at the castle. Otherwise. Well, you don't want to know. Got it?'

'And by what means are you maintaining a consistent threat against my very good friend?' asked the Patient.

'You know perfectly well,' said Winnifred. 'My knife and me make a fearsome partnership.'

'Your knife? Which knife would that be?' he asked.

'This one,' she replied, reaching to her side where she expected to find it tucked into her belt. It was missing. 'What the hell?'

'Ratty, I advise you most vehemently to run away without delay. It will take Winnifred a few moments to work out where I have secreted her knife, and by then the nurses will have alerted the hospital security staff, so I will be safe.'

Ratty tried not to look as disappointed as he felt. The concept of being kidnapped was frankly rather exciting. Running away did not have the same appeal.

'Let's not be hasty,' he said, 'for whilst I applaud your intentions and your rapid actions, Patient chappy, I really don't think these charming ladies mean to harm me. Perhaps we could do the kidnapping thing but without the knife? Just a kind of gentleman's agreement doodah. What do you say, ladies?'

'No one makes a fool out of me,' Winnifred hissed at the Patient. 'Just because I saved your ass doesn't mean I won't kick it. You understand?'

'Explicitly,' the Patient replied. 'Though if I may say so, your defensiveness and lack of good humour suggest an unresolved inferiority complex. Would you care to tell me about your childhood? Maybe we can get to the bottom of some of the issues that seem to be causing you problems in adulthood.'

'Fuck you, asshole. Where's my damn knife?'

'Excellent. That is a perfect representation of the kind of attitude that your condition can be expected to present. I think I have a clear idea of your psychological state, and I think I possess the means to cure it.'

'Never mind the knife,' suggested Ratty. 'Why don't we tootle off and wait for the others to find the treasure?'

'If I may be so bold,' added the Patient, 'there is another flaw in your plan, ladies. If your ransom is not a specific amount, merely the sum of whatever Saunière's treasure may happen to come to, which nobody knows, then how would you know if the treasure that eventually reaches you is the full quantity available?'

'Good point, Patient chappy. It seems to me as though this kidnapping malarkey is not as viable as we initially thought.'

'You're forgetting one thing, bozos,' grunted Winnifred, lifting the sheets and retrieving her knife from beneath the protective arch over the Patient's legs. 'The power of fear.' She pointed the knife towards Ratty. 'The kidnapping will go as planned. And if anyone keeps back so much as a penny of Saunière's money, Ratty gets it. Right?'

'The penny?' asked Ratty.

'Let's go,' said Justina, suppressing a sigh.

They nudged Ratty to another corridor lined with doors leading to private rooms. As they neared the far end, a door opened beside them. They looked around and Justina's eyes met with those of Henri, the Templar. He was bloodied and bruised, limping and dirty, but he was mobile and walked towards them unaided.

'A certain brevity in our step might be advisable,' whispered Ratty.

'Shh,' said Justina, walking towards the Templar. 'You're alive. What happened?'

'Compared to what is about to happen, nothing.'

*　*　*

Convinced that Ratty was no longer in the town, Ruby declared a pause to their search and invited Scabies to a café in the main square. This area had remained safely above the water line even while the river was at its most swollen. Here, life continued normally, other than for the excessive presence of firemen and *gendarmes*, plus a newly arrived television news team. She ordered coffees and croissants and they watched the unusually busy world around them.

'Come on Ruby, what would you do?'

'About what?'

'Put yourself in Saunière's shoes. You've got money you shouldn't have. The Vatican is breathing down your neck. You've got Calvé up the spout in Paris and she's going to have the brat. You can't stick around Rennes any more because it's getting too dodgy. So you fuck off to Switzerland to get some of your dosh. Where do you go from there? What do you do in 1917 with all the money you could hope for?'

'Bearing in mind that the north of France is off-limits with the war, and the south of France is equally risky for him because of his past, that still leaves a huge swathe of land in which to occupy himself. And that's assuming he doesn't go abroad.'

'Forget the location, Ruby. What would you *do* in his situation? You're pissed off. Resentful towards the Vatican.'

'I see where you're heading. Right, so if the Vatican gave me a hard time, I'd consider a way to get revenge. If only for fun.'

'Cool. Me too. I can think of a hundred ways to have that kind of fun.'

'And then I'd want to see the kid,' she said.

'The kid? You think he'd give a shit about it?'

'It's a human impulse. Of course he'd want to see it. He would also want to set the child up financially. He would find a way to ensure his wealth was channelled towards the kid after he was gone. And that's the tricky thing when you're dealing with money from iffy sources being handed over by someone who is officially dead and whose job ought to preclude him from fatherhood in the first place. How would he get that arranged?'

'We need to know who he could have trusted,' said Scabies. 'A friend, a lawyer, another priest, a family member?'

'A secret society with a similar grudge against the Vatican?' suggested Ruby.

'You mean like the Templars?'

'I mean the Templars. Precisely.'

'You think they might have been involved since he was still alive?' asked Scabies.

'It's possible, but we don't have much to go on. I hate it when historical research is based on wild speculation. We have to get some facts to build our hypothesis. All we've done since we got here is run around chasing our tails and getting nowhere. Randomly charging in and out of old tunnels is pointless. Any existing tunnel can only lead to somewhere that's already been plundered, if indeed it ever contained anything. I know you think it's fun to explore them, and they have historical merit in a sense, but they are a distraction. The Templars wouldn't keep a valuable hoard in Rennes. If they've been guarding it for almost a century, they would have moved it out of the village the moment the treasure hunters started using dynamite in the sixties. They're hardly likely to sit around and wait for someone to find it.'

'Unless they kept a close eye on everything, making sure no one got too close with their tunnels, and then they introduced the ban on excavations in 1965 and from then on they could relax.'

'But we all know the ban didn't stop the digging,' said Ruby. 'It merely drove it underground, if you'll forgive the pun. Everyone just carried on discreetly. That bloke, what did they call him? The mole. You told me all about him. He was tunnelling right up until he died a few years back, convinced he was about to discover a major religious artefact.'

'Yeah,' said Scabies, 'and you can take your pick of those round here. We've got holy grails, Mary Magdalenes, the ark of the covenant and a couple of

Jesuses. It all depends whose book you read. Plus there's the lost treasure of Jerusalem, the Cathars' hidden gold, and one or two other fortunes sitting around in the caves and the crypts. I wouldn't be surprised if someone claimed Lord Lucan and Amelia Earhart were hiding in the woods round here, too. And don't forget the aliens. This place has it all. Only trouble is, no one's ever found any of them.'

'Which is what I tried to explain to Ratty all along. But when his head fills with ideas about treasure he becomes unstoppable.'

'So we've established,' said Scabies, 'that the Templars may or may not be guarding Saunière's money, and that they might be keeping it somewhere around here or in any other part of the world. So that narrows it down a bit.'

'Sometimes I wish I did something normal for a living. This is impossible.'

'And it's not a living.'

'I wish I could just be a tourist,' she continued, 'passing by without getting involved. It never seems to work out that way.'

'Let's go to Vatican City and eat pasta and ice cream and take photos and do nothing else.'

Ruby sat upright, and planted her coffee cup on the table with excessive force.

'The Vatican. I should have thought of it earlier!'

'Thought of what?' asked Scabies.

'We need facts, right? And we have none. But that's because we're looking at this back to front.'

'Back to front? You mean we should look at Saunière's arse?'

'Shut up, moron. Listen. We both agreed that Saunière might have had a motive to play out some kind of revenge on the Vatican after he faked his death, OK?'

'Sure.'

'And that is nothing more than idle speculation on our part based on circumstantial evidence. In fact, there's not even circumstantial evidence, just ideas based on very little. But there's something we can do if we come at the problem the other way. All we have to do is check established historical facts in relation to the Vatican from 1917 onwards. If anyone threw rocks at it, rang its doorbell and ran away, poisoned the water, put rats down the Pope's cassock, started rumours or anything else, that should be our starting point. We will then be investigating from an established fact, and we may then find that the trail points back to Saunière or the Templars. It's a long shot, but at least it follows better principles than all this dumb tunnelling.'

Scabies' eyes lit up. He knew she was right. This might be the best chance of advancement in the mystery of Saunière that anyone had made in years.

'We need the Internet,' he said. 'Our phones are fucked. There's not a decent library for miles and half the phone lines in this valley were knocked out by the storm, so we're not going to get online here anyway.'

'Maybe we don't need the Internet,' said Ruby.

'I think you'll find we do.'

'You're forgetting our secret weapon. The walking, talking Wikipedia that is the Patient.'

'Only without so much of the walking.'

'Drink up. We need to pay him a visit in hospital. Where do you think they took him?'

'It would have to be Quillan,' said Scabies. 'Whenever I got smashed up after a drink and a fight in Rennes, I'd always wake up in Quillan.'

'I really don't want to know,' said Ruby, waving at the waiter for the bill.

***

The reception desk at the hospital in Quillan was not adequate to cope with the exceptional number of visitors. The glass shelf on which enquirers would lean looked as if it might shatter under the weight of elbows. Rocco looked at Charlie.

'We should see the Patient later, when it's not so busy,' said Rocco. 'Let's get on with what we're supposed to be doing and find who the Templars hired to flatten Ratty's home. It sounds much more fun than waiting in this queue.'

'I don't understand queues,' said Charlie. 'I believe in every man for himself. Survival of the fattest. I can find the Patient. Follow me.'

They squeezed past the line of relatives waiting to find where their injured loved ones were located, turned a corner and found a staircase.

'He won't be on the ground floor,' said Rocco. 'Patient wards are always upstairs in buildings like this.'

On the next level they found a nurse.

'No Charlie,' said Rocco, 'don't ask that question.'

'Can you tell me where I can find the Patient?' sniggered Charlie.

'Yes?' answered the nurse.

'You just had to try it, didn't you?' said Rocco.

'Felt good. It's OK. We can go now. Let's just check each ward until we find him.'

'Wait,' said the nurse. 'Do you mean the man with the leg injuries who calls himself the Patient?'

'Yes,' Rocco replied, eager for news. 'Is he OK? Where is he?'

'Right here,' she answered, pointing to the centre of the ward behind her.

'Here?' asked Charlie, failing to spot the Patient.

The nurse looked around. The bed she was pointing at was empty. 'That's impossible,' she replied. 'He cannot walk. And he was here just a few minutes ago.'

Rocco sprinted to the far end of the ward, checking behind its closed door.

'Bathroom?' asked Charlie.

'He has a bedpan,' the nurse explained.

'Gross. Did you give him a wheelchair?'

'Of course not. He's just had a complex and delicate operation on his legs. He needs complete rest for at least two weeks so the bone can start to heal around the pins.'

Rocco ran back to them. 'Nothing. I checked behind the curtains and doors. He's gone.'

The nurse inspected the empty bed. 'It is his bed. No one has wheeled him away in it.'

'Could he drag himself to a wheelchair and use that?' asked Rocco.

'The pain would be unbearable,' the nurse replied.

'But he's just had surgery,' said Rocco. 'The anaesthetic will mask the pain, at least for a few more hours.'

***

The Patient was counting on the same theory. His legs were numb weights, useless, providing him with nothing but a dull ache. He was perfectly aware of the medical implications of forgoing the prescribed bed rest he was due. The list of risks to which he was now exposed was long, ranging from mild side-effects such as bending the metal pins in his femur which could lead to a curvature of the bone when it started to heal, all the way to potentially lethal complications including the rupture of an artery from the uncontrolled movement of unfused chunks of metal and bone.

With a blanket on his lap to hide his hospital robe, he had pushed himself determinedly in the wheelchair straight to the elevator and down to the busy reception hall where kind strangers had helped him through the main doors to the road. In his haste he had actually arrived outside ahead of the Templar he was attempting to follow. He reversed himself against the wall and waited for the injured man to limp through the door. No one paid any attention to the lone wheelchair user, and when Ratty, Winnifred and Justina emerged seconds later, followed by the Templar, they didn't notice him either. A shape in the Templar's pocket suggested a gun was being employed. The Patient knew instantly that was the focus of their attention.

He waited until the party had walked a reasonable distance ahead of him before pushing himself along in pursuit. Every bump in the path rocked his delicate legs. The sensation was not painful, but he could tell that his nerves were attempting to inform him of the crisis they were suffering.

At the car park he paused. The Templar waited with his hostages. The Patient was incredulous. A kidnapping was taking place in which the criminal was waiting for a ride. Taxi or colleague, he wasn't sure. He wheeled himself as close as possible without revealing his presence to them.

A car arrived and halted in front of the Templar. He pushed Ratty and the women into the back, then climbed stiffly into the front passenger seat. The Patient inched closer and memorised the licence plate, make, model, colour and distinguishing marks of the vehicle. It was a black BMW 740i bearing an '11' plate to show it was from the local region, Aude. He couldn't see the driver clearly. Still, assuming he could gain access to the appropriate police database, he was confident of tracing the address to which the car was registered.

His legs were throbbing more consistently now. He wheeled himself back towards the hospital building, repeating the number plate of the car in his head until it was as familiar as an old friend. He needed to return to his bed and lay his legs out straight. And he needed painkillers. Lots of them. He could sense every agonising screw, every crack, every gap and every damaged muscle in his legs. His synapses shrieked with pain so frequently that everything started to merge into an agony that was without end. He closed his eyes, trying to focus his mind away from these feelings, but instead of decreasing, they worsened. Seconds later his brain threw in the towel and he passed out.

**

'Impressive motor car,' said Ratty as they sped along the twisting country roads. 'Must have cost quite a few of those little Euro wotsits. Very refined engine. Seems built for this kind of road. Is it your vehicle – I'm sorry, I don't know your name,' he said, addressing the driver, who gave no response. 'Or is it a company car?' This time he interpreted the silence to mean something. 'I was wondering what is the name of your organisation. Must be fairly well off to have transport like this for its staff.'

'I know who you are,' said the Templar.

'Jolly good,' replied Ratty. 'Marvellous. Tremendous. So nice to know I haven't been spirited away at random.'

'I know your identity,' continued the Templar, 'but the question remains, do you?'

'Do I what?'

'Do you know your true identity?'

'Got it written down somewhere. So many names I can never remember them all. Ballashiels, St Clair, Lord this, that and the other, Justin, one or two other bits and pieces. Far easier to stick with Ratty. Everyone does.'

The car stopped at the entrance to a remote olive farm clinging to the side of a steep hill.

'I know this place,' said Justina. 'If you carry on up the hill it leads to Bézu peak. It's an old Templar lookout point. Used to be a little castle or something there. It looks out across the valley at Rennes-le-Château.'

'So you Templar chappies are still doing your wotsits up here, eh?' asked Ratty.

'We do as we have always done,' said the driver. 'We know who we are and we know why we are.'

'Always advisable,' Ratty said, and climbed out at the invitation of the Templar.

***

'Hey, Mr Victim!'

'Shh,' whispered Ruby. 'Let's get him inside. He needs help.'

'Nah, he's just sleeping,' said Scabies. 'Probably tired after all that excitement this morning.'

The Patient's eyes flickered. As they stabilised and stayed open, his face twisted with pain.

'Look at him,' said Ruby. 'He needs painkillers.'

'No time,' whispered the Patient. 'Ratty has been taken. We have to find him.'

'But, *why* would anyone want to take him?' asked Scabies. 'What's he useful for?'

The Patient tried to speak, but couldn't overcome the pain shooting through his legs. Ruby couldn't watch him suffer like that and pushed him into the building in search of drugs. While she spent time explaining the apparent situation to a nurse, Scabies slipped into a stock room and emerged with a vial of morphine and a set of syringes. He found Ruby in the middle of an argument with the nurse, who refused to provide any pain relief to the Patient until he had been seen by a doctor. Scabies whispered in Ruby's ear. She smiled and simply walked away from the nurse, pushing the Patient before her.

'How did you find the drugs cupboard so quickly?'

'I told you. I've been here many times before.'

Ruby prepared a measure of morphine in a syringe as they stood at the side of the car park.

'You ready, Patient?'

'I should probably perform the injection,' he replied. 'I appreciate that you are a doctor of sorts, Ruby, but I know that archaeological medicine is concerned with those who are already dead, not with the living.' He took the syringe from her and jabbed himself in the upper thigh. Seconds later the stress lines vanished from his face and he breathed deeply.

'Feeling better?' asked Scabies. 'Don't you go becoming a junkie as well as a victim, right?'

'I have memorised the registration number,' said the Patient, ignoring Scabies. 'We must access the police database immediately. Ratty is in danger. Let's take a taxi to the police station.'

'Yeah, I'm not sure that's the best thing to do,' said Scabies. 'The police might have some difficult questions for us.'

'Shit,' said Ruby. 'But we have to do something. Even if we risk getting arrested ourselves. We have to help Ratty.'

'I have a solution,' said the Patient. 'If we can't ask the police for the information, we can make them give it away without realising.'

'And how do you propose to do that?' asked Ruby.

'It's shockingly easy,' replied the Patient. 'If you report their registration number and claim they failed to stop after running me over, the police will go to their address. And if we wait near the police station with our engine running, we can follow them there. All the way to their hideout.'

'Right, with our engine running ...' said Scabies. 'Which engine would that be?'

'Take your pick of the staff cars,' said the Patient. 'Choose a car from the staff section of the car park and I will tell you how to open it and get it started, but you must do as I say: I cannot contribute any physical labour.'

Half an hour later they waited outside the police station in a stolen Renault Clio that they guessed belonged to a nurse and which, if luck was on their side, would not get reported stolen for a few more hours. Ruby had made the hit-and-run call and it was just a matter of seeing which direction the next car would head off to and then following it.

'What if they send a car that's already out on patrol?' Ruby asked.

'No plan is perfect,' replied the Patient from his reclined position across the back seat.

'While we're waiting,' said Ruby, 'we were talking about what Saunière might have done after January 1917. We think he might have tried to take some kind of revenge on the Vatican, and we wondered if you had read about anything like that. Something that might have happened from 1917 onwards?'

'Of course,' the Patient replied.

'That was quick,' said Scabies, tapping his fingers on the steering wheel as he waited to spot a police car. 'What was the little scamp doing, then?'

'There is no written evidence for Saunière's involvement in this, but later in 1917 there was the Fatima event.'

'Fatima? Who was she?' asked Ruby.

'I can tell you're not Catholic,' said Scabies.

'Fatima is a town in Portugal,' explained the Patient. 'A young girl reported seeing the Virgin Mary and being told three secrets about the future. It was widely reported as a miracle. The first two secrets were said to predict world wars, and the third one was suppressed for decades. This third secret is said to have predicted the downfall of the Vatican, the murder of a pope, and a fundamental shift away from allowing the church to dictate to its brethren in favour of a more direct and personal approach to a relationship with God.'

'Interesting,' said Ruby. 'There's no such thing as a miracle, so either the girl invented the whole thing or she was fooled into believing what she saw, even though it might have been faked.'

'Saunière in a dress?' asked Scabies.

'He was wealthy, remember. He could afford an actress, costumes, even primitive special effects. I'm not saying he did, I'm just saying it's possible. Or the Templars might have helped him. Right?'

'Sure,' said Scabies. 'A practical joke, I suppose. Never did get French humour. Making the Vatican think their days were numbered is pretty cool. Might give that a try some time.'

'Fatima is a possible link,' said Ruby, 'and it's somewhere he could have spent his last years in hiding – reasonable climate, two countries away from France – but I just don't think it fits what we know about him. Saunière built a castle as his study. Most people use a spare room or a shed. He spent a fortune on personal construction projects to impress his visitors. We're talking serious ego, here. He's not the kind of character that wants to hide in remote Portugal. He must have gone to Paris. And if not Paris, then …' She paused, wondering if anyone else might be thinking along the same lines.

'London,' beamed the Patient, slipping into a deeply relaxing catatonic state.

'Police car,' said Scabies, pulling away after it. 'Here we go.'

Charlie and Rocco emerged through the hospital doors. They were sweating and agitated.

'What is it with this Patient dude?' shouted Charlie. 'We've searched every room. How can he just disappear when he's got no damn legs?'

'Forget about him, Charlie. There's nothing we can do. He might have been transferred to another hospital, or he might have died. Either way we can't help him right now. Let's get a cab into town and find that address in the Templar notebook.'

They walked to the taxi rank and read the address to the driver. Rue de la Mairie wasn't far. When they arrived, Charlie looked up and down the picturesque street, a narrow terrace of ancient townhouses with wooden shutters painted in bright blues and yellows, broken up by cafés and antique shops and window boxes bursting with blooms. He found it hard to believe that the hired thug they were looking for would live in such a pretty street.

'This is the place,' said Rocco, looking at the small plaque adjacent to the door. It had a name engraved on it: 'A. Boyer'. The name matched the handwritten scrawl in the notebook, but the modest nameplate gave no hint as to the person's profession. The building was well maintained, its cerulean-painted shutters were open, and loud guitar music escaped from an open window.

'What if he's violent?' asked Charlie. 'I'm not sure this is a good idea.'

'He can't be any bigger than you. So what is there to be scared of?'

'We don't have weapons. I didn't bring my sword.'

'We don't need swords, Charlie. A mindless brute like this can easily be outsmarted by a superior intellect.'

'Huh?'

Rocco pressed the buzzer. The music stopped mid-riff.

'*Oui*?' came a high-pitched voice from the intercom. Charlie relaxed.

'Stiperstones Manor,' Rocco replied, curtly.

'OK,' the voice answered.

There was a buzz and a click. Rocco pushed the door open and led the way inside. They could hear footsteps thumping down the tiled stairs towards them.

'*Oui*?' repeated the short, brown-haired girl standing before them, Fender Stratocaster in hand.

'You speak English?' asked Rocco, for Charlie's benefit.

'Of course,' she replied. 'We do have schools in this country, you know.'

'Right. Well, we're looking for Monsieur Boyer. Is he home?'

'There is no one of that name here. Who are you?'

'There is according to the plaque next to your door,' said Rocco.

'And where does it say *Monsieur*?' she asked, her attitude making her seem taller than she was.

Rocco stepped outside and looked again. She was right. There was no indication of whether the person named on the sign was male or female.

'You are A. Boyer?' he asked, closing the door behind him.

'*Oui*. I am Aurelia. And you are?'

'I'm Rocco. This is Charlie.'

'Pleased to meet you,' Aurelia told them. 'And you want to talk to me about Stiperstones?'

'If you have a few minutes, yes,' said Rocco.

'Won't you come in?' She led the way up the steps to her living room. A sofa was hiding beneath loose throws and a couple of cats. A coffee table was littered with laptops and coffee mugs and a paperback copy of *So Long, and Thanks for all the Fish*. A Marshall stack hummed softly in the centre of the room, waiting for reconnection with the guitar. 'It's not tidy. I am too busy composing. There is no time for housework when you are creating music.'

'Composing?' asked Charlie. 'Like, songwriting?'

She nodded and studied her visitors. They were unshaven, their clothes were stained with mud, and their hair was unkempt. They smelled as bad as they looked.

'You can sit on the sofa with the cats,' she told them.

They sat down. No one said anything. Charlie stroked the cat nearest to him and it hissed.

'Aurelia, thank you for speaking to us. We want to find out about the work you have done for the Templars, with regard to Stiperstones. Can you tell us about that?'

'Why? What is your interest?'

'We're friends of the owner of the house,' Rocco told her. 'Lord Ballashiels has received an unsettling letter regarding his property and I wanted to know if there was any substance behind it and whether you have any connection to it.'

'Of course I do,' she replied.

'I don't mean to be rude, but how come someone like you is involved in all this?'

'Someone like me? You don't know anything about me.'

'I mean someone so young. How old are you?'

'I may be small but I am not a child. I am almost twenty-two.'

'OK, but to be working for a secret society? Do you even know who you've been dealing with?'

'I am not stupid,' she stated. 'And it is not as if I had any choice.'

'Have they threatened you? Did they hurt you?'

'Why would they do that? I am a songwriter. I do freelance marketing to make extra money. And if my father asks me to help with a publicity and information campaign, I would never refuse him.'

'You're a freelance publicist? Is that all?'

'We thought you were some kind of tough guy, hitman dude,' said Charlie, unable to drag his eyes away from her.

'And clearly you were mistaken,' she replied. 'Listen, my work for my father—'

'Wait, did you say "father"?' asked Rocco.

'Yes. He is a Templar. I sometimes do work for him and some of the other guys in their silly club.'

'Silly club?' asked Rocco. 'I never expected to hear it called that. You're talking about the most powerful, the most feared, and probably the wealthiest organisation in the whole of France. And who is your father?'

'He is Monsieur Boyer. Surely that is not a surprise?'

'Ah, sure. That works,' said Charlie.

'As I tried to explain before, the nature of my work for him and his organisation has always been secret. I'm afraid I can't disclose any of it, other than to say I think it's all pointless what they get up to. But if you have something you want to tell me about Stiperstones Manor, then I am happy to listen.'

'Well,' said Rocco, 'only that it would be really helpful if you could make sure that it doesn't get destroyed, if that is within your power.'

'Do I look like a destroyer of buildings?'

'With that Marshall stack you could probably turn it to dust with a loud solo,' said Charlie, as if he would like to try such a thing himself. 'Does it go up to eleven?'

'Any other dumb questions?'

'Only to ask if your father is OK after last night's storm?' said Rocco.

'Why would you ask me that? Why would he not be?'

'You didn't hear about the flood?'

'Yes, but it's happened before. We are used to it.'

'I heard that a Templar house was destroyed in Rennes-les-Bains.'

'So? Bricks can be rebuilt. My father does not live there, anyway.' Despite her bravado she looked concerned.

'Have you heard from him today?' asked Rocco.

'No. Just been writing songs all day.'

'So you didn't hear about the car crash last night?'

'What are you talking about?'

'A car hit a fallen tree just outside Rennes-les-Bains. This notebook was inside.'

Aurelia snatched it from Rocco's hands. 'Let me see!' she shouted, her veins starting to flood her with the colour of anxiety. 'This is my father's notebook. How did you get it?'

'We found it in the smashed up car this morning,' said Rocco. 'But we don't know where he went. It's possible someone took him to the hospital already, since the car was empty when we found it.'

'Please go. Now. I have to find my father.'

'Yes, of course. But we can help you find him.'

'How? You don't even know where he lives. Do you have a car?'

'Not any more,' said Charlie.

'Do you have any idea where to look for him?' she sighed.

'Since you must know his address,' said Rocco, 'yes I do: I would simply ask you. But first we need to check out the hospitals.'

'Why are you so stupid? First I will just telephone him. Be quiet, both of you.'

She picked up her iPhone and walked into the kitchen. Rocco overheard the word '*Papa*' but couldn't make out anything more from the hushed conversation. When she returned a minute later her demeanour had changed. The carefree twenty-two-year-old was now an adult bowing beneath a heavy burden.

'My uncle is dead,' she mumbled. 'Papa is hurt. And he tells me you are connected to these things.'

***

Scabies parked at the base of the hill among the olive trees and climbed out.

'Why have you stopped?' Ruby asked. 'The police car is out of sight. We've lost it.'

'Come on, hurry up. I know this road. It's a dead end. Just leads to the olive farm and on to the ruins of the old Templar outpost at Bézu. So the police must be going to the farm.'

'Wait. What about the Patient?'

'He's asleep. Leave him in the back.'

'But the olive trees aren't giving enough shade. You're parked half in the sun. If dogs can die in hot cars, so can he!'

'So leave the windows open and give him a bowl of water. Come on!'

With the engine off the electric windows wouldn't move, so Ruby simply left the passenger door wide open. She jogged up the hill towards Scabies.

'Look. That's the police car through the trees.' She pointed towards the track leading to the farmhouse. 'Let's stop them when they leave and tell them about the kidnapping.'

'So why didn't you report a kidnapping to start with instead of a hit and run?'

'I suppose I didn't want Ratty to get mixed up with the police, given his situation in England with the body they found in his house.'

'Right. I get that. So in that case, we wait until the police leave, then we go in alone and find Ratty.'

'You think it's that easy to foil a kidnapping plot?'

'Ruby, anything is easy when you've made a career out of playing drums while they're on fire. We go round the back of the farmhouse, find a way in, find which room they're keeping him in, then get him out and back to the car.'

'And nothing can go wrong,' said Ruby, clearly thinking the opposite.

'Why do you have to be such a pessimist? If they see us, just use that irresistible feminine charm of yours.'

'Go fuck yourself.'

'That's the stuff!'

***

The farmhouse library – though smaller in proportion – felt homely to Ratty. The bookcases were made from mahogany, just like at Stiperstones. The faded parquet floor shared the same scratches and patches as his home. The unlit fireplace was framed by stonework equal in grandeur and craftsmanship to the mantels he was used to. The sole alienating difference was the books. Whilst Ratty took pride in surrounding himself with the entire canon of classic English literature, every book in this library was French, scarred by aesthetically displeasing spines whose titles ran bottom to top instead of in the correct direction.

He attempted to drink the tea he had been given. It grated his taste buds as badly as the books offended his eyes. Maybe he was imagining it. The DNA swab he had been unexpectedly forced to rub around the inside of his mouth might have left an aftertaste that disagreed with the tea. Far from being the civilised hospitality intended by his host, Ratty was experiencing a multi-sensory assault. Still, considering he had been kidnapped by Winnifred and Justina, and that all three of them had subsequently been whisked away at gunpoint by the Templars, he figured things could have been worse. He had seen nothing of the women since their arrival at the olive farm. The Templar had put him in the library with a pot of not-quite-tea and taken the Americans elsewhere, and now he waited.

He twitched when the door handle turned slowly. A dribble of brown liquid slid down the outside of his cup, into the saucer. He put the beverage on the table and stood up to greet the Templar.

'Please sit,' said the Templar, limping towards him and pointing at the chair where Ratty had previously sat. The Templar eased himself onto one of the chairs opposite. 'Don't worry about the women. They are safe.'

Ratty had no concerns whatsoever for their safety.

'That is a welcome unburdening,' he said. 'Look, I don't mean to be ungrateful for the hospitality, but the council bulldozers have a rendezvous with my home in a couple of days and I really ought to go and lie down in the mud in front of them.'

'These things do not occur without good reason. And I am sorry for making you wait. I just had a visit from the *gendarmes* of Quillan. They do an excellent job, but this was a small misunderstanding which I was able to straighten out without difficulty.'

'*Gendarme* chappies? Did you offer them tea? I would be willing to sacrifice my own pot in the interests of community wotnots.'

'That will not be necessary. They have already departed. Now, the reason you are here is because we are in a very fast-moving, quickly evolving situation,' said the Templar. 'Yesterday's enemy is today's friend. Do you understand?'

'No at all, old onion.'

'Let me explain.' He adjusted his legs to make his recent injuries more bearable. 'For many years people have investigated the so-called treasure of Bérenger Saunière. It has come in and out of fashion. Many books were written, holes were dug, and lives were dedicated to finding his secret. All wasted, of course. And all because the villagers of his day didn't understand the source of his money and so they started to spread rumours of treasure. And human nature being what it is, when those rumours start they never go away.'

'So where did the old fellow find—'

'Don't ask,' interrupted the Templar. 'What I am saying is that no one ever came remotely close to the truth before. And then suddenly, with no warning, everything happens at once. The Marsaud family are murdered. One of the suspects claims descent from Saunière. You arrive on the scene. Rennes-les-Bains is destroyed by floods. My brother is killed in a car accident. And you force us into a corner until we have no options remaining.'

'Golly. Frightfully regrettable. My deepest doodahs and dingdangs. Thing is, not quite sure how I forced you to do anything when I didn't know you existed.'

'Your ignorance is understandable, but you know us. We are in your soul.'

'Are you? Are you indeed? In my soul, eh? Thought it was a bit crowded in there, actually.'

'You know Saunière left Rennes in 1917, don't you? You know he was alive for many years after. No other researchers noticed this until you. That is how you have cornered us.'

'Still not a hundred per cent with you, old baguette.'

'The question we must ask is how? How did you find this out? Because of all the secrets of Saunière, the knowledge of his lost years is the greatest.'

'Gosh, well, just a little coincidence, really. That Charlie Chaplin fellow—'

The Templar stood up, looking frightened, then winced as the pain in his leg reminded him of his current frailty. 'The Chaplin conspiracy! Well, Lord Ballashiels, I am even more impressed by your ingenuity. You cultivate your image of stupidity very well, and you use it to mask your true genius. I must admire your tactics.' With that, he sat back down again.

'Quite. Yes. The Chaplin thingummy. That's the fellow.'

'Chaplin is a French name, you know.'

'No one's perfect.'

'It is from the old French word, *chapelain*. A chaplain. A priest. Do you see?'

'See what, old croissant?'

'It was Saunière's habit to leave clues, and with the Charlie Chaplin connection he created the biggest, highest profile clue of them all, and for almost a century no one spotted it, even though it was so open and blatant. Until you, Lord Ballashiels. I must congratulate you for being able to see the wood for the trees. Tell me, how did you work it out?'

'Elementary, my dear Wotsname.'

'It is so elementary, you are right, but only the clearest mind can see past the nonsense that distracts all others who seek the truth.'

'So when I saw Charlie Doodah and the Saunière fellow filmed at Rennes-le-Whatsit together, all the pieces in the thingummy fitted and I realised I knew everything,' lied Ratty, trying to live up to his unexpected reputation for cognitive prowess.

'And yet, and this is the part that is hard for me to comprehend, you then came to Rennes and started poking around in the tunnels,' said the Templar. 'Why?'

'Agoraphobia,' said Ratty. 'Never did trust open spaces.'

'And I find you getting mixed up with those American women, one of whom, it seems, was responsible for multiple murders while the other claims to be related to Saunière and Calvé.'

'I can explain about the drummer chap, and the archaeologist, and the peculiar Patient fellow. To some extent I can even explain about the rotund young American and the paranoid German scientist, but I must confess that the American ladies just kind of appeared in my life a couple of days ago and for some reason have refused to depart.'

'Ah, yes, I am beginning to see the light. I expected you to travel across the Atlantic upon learning of the Chaplin conspiracy. But that is too obvious, isn't it?'

'Quite. Too expensive, if anything.'

'You didn't go to America. You let America come to you. That's it, isn't it? Those women are part of the conspiracy? That's why they're here!'

Ratty didn't know what to say. He had ceased to comprehend anything the Templar had been saying several minutes ago. He just nodded politely and pretended to take a sip of the vile tea. 'Do you have a gentleman's room?' he asked.

'Of course,' said the Templar. 'Before you go, I want you to be reassured. What you have revealed to me has saved the lives of those two women. You should feel very proud. Obviously there is some paperwork to sort out, but I can see a resolution to the Saunière legacy at last.'

***

With her nose pressed against the cobwebs, Ruby could see into the unlit barn at the rear of the imposing farmhouse. The barn was used for storing vats of olive oil, rows of metal drums containing extra virgin pressings of an as-yet unbranded variety. She turned to face Scabies, who was still crouched behind the tractor that had concealed him from the departing police, and held up her thumb. He approached the barn door. It refused to open. He shook his head at her and she joined him, huffing disapprovingly.

'How many drummers does it take to change a lightbulb?' asked Ruby. 'One. If you hit it hard enough it should just work.'

'How many archaeologists does it take to piss off a drummer?' he retorted. 'One. You.' He kicked the door in using a move he had perfected years before when booting burning floor toms off the stage. 'Come on.'

They squeezed past rows of olive oil containers.

'Does this look like the headquarters of a wealthy and influential secret society?' whispered Ruby. 'The farmhouse is pretty imposing, but this is a working barn. Just as if it's a real olive farm.'

'That's exactly what they want you to think.'

Scabies approached a heavy-looking door at the rear of the barn. He put his face to the door's tiny window and gave Ruby a thumbs up.

'What does that mean?' she asked. 'You can see Ratty? The coast is clear? You've spotted a drum set?'

He turned to her and sighed. 'Kit, Ruby. They're called kits.'

'I'm just saying that sticking your thumb up doesn't tell me enough about—'

'It was good enough for you just now!'

'But that situation was different. No ambiguity.'

'Agh! All right, I get it! Look for yourself!'

He stood aside and let her peek through. She could see a kitchen: worktops of green tiles with chequered curtains beneath, butler sink, flagstone floor, pine table and chairs, wood-burning stove. The only nod to modernity seemed to be the fridge, and even that could have been thirty years old.

Scabies pushed the door. The hinges squealed, as if deliberately attempting to raise the alarm. With the door only ajar, he paused. 'Too loud,' he whispered.

'You don't say,' came Ruby's reply.

'Wait here.' He looked around the barn until he found a stack of boxes. Inside the top box he found bottles of the farm's produce, extra virgin olive oil. He took a bottle and opened it, pouring a drop onto his hands to taste.

'Is it real?' asked Ruby.

'Yes and no,' Scabies replied. 'Try it.'

He poured a drop onto her fingers and she licked them.

'Eek,' was her reaction. 'Rancid.'

'That's what I thought. It's olive oil all right,' he said, 'but it's been sitting here a few years. Doesn't matter. Watch.'

He sprinkled the ancient oil onto the hinges and tried pushing the door again. This time it swung open in reassuring silence. Scabies put the bottle into his pocket in case they encountered any other sticky doors.

They stepped into the rustic kitchen. In the centre sat a wonky table dressed with a couple of baguettes. Scabies went instinctively to the little fridge that hummed in the corner and opened it. '*Fromage*?' he offered.

'No time,' she replied, snapping off the end of a baguette and stuffing it into her mouth.

'They've got both kinds of cheese,' he continued. 'Camembert *and* Brie.'

Ruby's mouth was too full to be able to articulate the sarcastic response she so wanted to utter, so she compromised with slapping Scabies on the arm and pushing him towards a door that led to a hallway.

The hallway was long and dark. It was lined with three doors on each side. All closed. They could hear voices. Scabies pressed his ear against each door in turn. At the second he gave a thumbs-down sign. At the next he smiled. The muffled tones of Ratty talking gibberish floated into the hallway.

'He's there?' whispered Ruby.

'Yes, but he's with someone.'

'We need to hide until he's alone.'

Before they could retreat to the kitchen, the door opened and Ratty emerged. He instantly shut the door behind him.

'Just looking for the gentleman's department,' he wibbled to Scabies.

'Ratty, listen, we've come to get you out of here,' Ruby spat into his ear, her words fractured by nervous excitement and pieces of baguette.

'Say again, old trout?'

'This way!' she summarised, grabbing his arm and guiding him to the kitchen. Scabies closed the door.

'By "gentlemen's department" I was really referring to the water closet,' said Ratty, looking confused to be in a kitchen. 'You know, to powder one's, you know. Without getting vulgar or too explicit. Unmentionables. If you'll forgive my—'

'Listen Ratty, we found out something,' interrupted Ruby. 'These Templars have been watching you for a long time. Your name and address were in a notebook we found in the car that chased us out of Rennes-les-Bains.'

'Yes, most amusing story, actually, because the Templar chap knew all about Charlie Chaplin and

Saunière. Only he went further to talk about Chaplin meaning *priest* and something about America and then quite frankly I felt a little light-headed and ceased to follow what he was saying. Let me introduce you to him. Charming fellow.'

'No, Ratty, we can't trust him. He was trying to kill us just twenty-four hours ago.'

'Oh, that's a bit of an exaggeration, don't you think?'

'No, Ratty. A bullet hit the camper van, remember?'

'I know, I meant it wasn't quite twenty-four hours – probably only about nineteen – but the Templar fellow explained all that, I think. Something about him realising all sorts of things, and people not being the enemies he originally considered them to be, and all that wizzle-wazzle.'

'Wizzle-wazzle?' repeated Scabies. 'Why did we ever get involved with this clown, Ruby?'

The kitchen door swung open to reveal the Templar, holding himself painfully upright against the frame. 'I thought I heard the sound of other guests,' he said, his voice lacking the sinister undertone that Ruby and Scabies were expecting. 'Don't be afraid of me. It was not me who shot at you yesterday. That man is dead. He was my brother. And it was I who killed him. Please sit. My stitches are painful.'

He limped to the kitchen table and pulled up a chair. The others joined him, self-consciously sticking to the opposite side of the table.

'Why did you bump your brother off?' asked Scabies. 'If it's not a personal question.'

'I was driving the car. It was not intentional. Likewise, I know his intention was not to hurt you. He was convinced you would stop if he frightened you. We were arguing about it. I told him he was reckless, this was not how we do things. I tried to pull the gun from his hand. Your van swerved suddenly into the river and I didn't have time to see the fallen tree in the road. He died at that moment and I woke up later in Quillan hospital. These are strange days. Much has changed and will change and must change. Lord Ballashiels is an undisputed genius. He has uncovered the Chaplin conspiracy. I am at once grateful and relieved that he has done so. It is the lifting of a burden that has been carried for too long.'

Ruby and Scabies looked quizzically at Ratty.

'Genius?' asked Scabies.

'Chaplin conspiracy?' asked Ruby.

'That's the fellow,' said Ratty. 'The wotsname thingummy. Worked it all out.'

'We are in the presence of greatness,' said the Templar. Scabies looked over his shoulder and around the room. 'And I recognise you, *Monsieur*. A face from my youth. Perhaps the greatest drummer on the planet?'

'Perhaps,' coughed Scabies, modestly. 'Certainly the greatest drummer in The Damned.'

'The *qui*?'

Scabies bit his lip tightly. Ratty brought the conversation back to topic.

'*Monsieur* Templar chappy, I have yet to acquaint my chums with the Charlie Chaplin conspiracy story and I wondered if you would do the honours, since you tell it with so much more *aplomb*, if you'll excuse my French.'

'I am sure you would prefer to explain the complex conspiracy which you have so brilliantly uncovered,' suggested the Templar. 'Go ahead. In your own words.'

'Ah. Words. Right. Speaking, no less. A fine oration is what you want. My best spiel. And why not? A not entirely unreasonable suggestion. Most laudable. However, if I may protrude an opinion into the general mêlée, I always think such a tale sounds more authentic with the amusing – I mean the appropriate – accent. An accent which, for various reasons including dignity, breeding and not smoking, I am unable to emulate.'

The smoking reference caused Scabies to produce a roll-up and a lighter from his pocket. Ruby slapped his arm, shook her head and mouthed the word 'outside'. He grunted and lowered his hands.

'You wish me to tell it for you?' asked the Templar.

'Hmm? Oh, why not. If you insist,' said Ratty.

'A pleasure,' the Templar replied. 'Saunière passed on in January 1917. We have his death certificate, the details of his burial, and there is even a photo of him on his deathbed in some books. But the certificate was signed by the mayor along with Pierre Captier and Louis Bousquet, a farmer and a builder. Is it feasible that these three men could have been paid off by Saunière for their complicity in aiding his escape from Rennes-le-Château during a time of extreme crisis for the priest? Well, I know that was the case. And we know too that the supposed deathbed photo was not even Saunière. Skip forward three months and there is a document from Limoux, registered by the clerk of the court, which proves that Saunière's brothers and sisters, the only known heirs to his considerable estate, declined their right to inherit. Is that not strange behaviour?'

'Most queersome,' said Ratty. 'I was going to mention the very same thing.'

'So Saunière's young housekeeper, Marie, continued living in his properties with her parents. Under French law, if the estate remained uncontested, she would inherit everything after thirty years. But that was just the bricks. Saunière had already given them up when he disappeared in 1917. Those rumours of treasure put about by ignorant villagers were a useful smokescreen, and one that he encouraged in order to draw attention away from his lucrative trade in mail order masses. He may have sold some gold along the way, treasures from a crypt or a tomb, but if that did happen it was an isolated event. No one else will find anything of value in the village.

'The fact is, when he started advertising to the faithful of the United States, the scale of his operation became vast. So huge, in fact, that he began to keep some of the money in America to invest in the New York Stock Exchange. It was partly his escape plan, and it was also because at one point he had no choice. The Vatican was putting pressure on the Bishop of Carcassonne, Beauséjour, to stop this errant priest. Saunière was constantly in trouble, on trial, and getting banned from the ministry. Whilst suspended from his job, he was not entitled to collect letters addressed to the *curé* of Rennes-le-Château from the post office at Couiza. His funds were cut off. So he hired a New York lawyer to invest the money for him, without it travelling to France.'

'More or less how I would have relayed the same story, only far more eloquent,' said Ratty.

'But Saunière was becoming addicted to his high-spending lifestyle and 1914 became a pivotal year for him.'

'I would have said critical,' said Ratty.

'It was pivotal,' continued the Templar. 'The start of the war in Europe resulted in financial panic across the world. The New York Stock Exchange was shut down for four months, right when Saunière needed to liquidate some stocks and send the funds over to France. He was broke. He had debts of thousands of Francs. His situation became serious. And that was when he made the decision that was to change everything.'

'Blackmail,' said Scabies.

'Of course,' said the Templar. 'To this day we don't know if he invented the story or if he genuinely found what he claimed to have discovered, but facing financial ruin and the loss of everything he had built throughout his life, he resorted to writing a letter to the new Pope, Benedict, requesting a sum of money to pay his reasonable expenses in the destruction and resealing of a tomb he had discovered in the vicinity of Rennes-le-Château which contained the remains of Mary Magdalene together with writings documenting her marriage to Jesus and their offspring. Despite the polite and elegant wording of this letter, its intent was clear. The sum of money he had requested was one million Francs. It was more than enough to last him the rest of his life, and would have funded all of the additional things he wanted to build, like the road to the village so he could buy a car, and a library tower far taller than the Tour Magdala that he had already constructed. And, most importantly, one million Francs was blatantly excessive for burning some papers and bricking up a hole. The Pope knew this was blackmail.'

'Wish I had a few Magdalenes under Stiperstones,' whispered Ratty. 'Could do with that kind of ransom.'

'So where does Charlie Chaplin come in?' asked Ruby.

'The Chaplin conspiracy was still some years away,' replied the Templar. 'The Pope called Saunière's bluff. The money wasn't paid. Vatican spies came to the village and started poking around for evidence to use against Saunière. Meanwhile he had re-established his trade in masses and was beginning to accumulate money once again. But he had done too much damage. He sensed a plot developing against him. The only permanent way out, he realised, was to be dead. And so he faked his death, intending to travel to America and live off his investments.'

'And I'm guessing that never happened?' asked Ruby.

'When does life ever go as planned?' asked the Templar. 'There were many complicating factors. He was resentful against the church for driving him away. As he saw it, sending him money for masses made people feel a sense of satisfaction. It didn't matter if he actually said them, which, of course, even with the additional years of his life that we know he had, would have been impossible given their large number.'

'He wanted to revenge the church,' said Ruby. 'I knew it. That's exactly what I said, didn't I?' Scabies nodded. 'Was it Fatima? Was the Patient right?'

This time the Templar nodded. 'He frightened them with predictions of their own demise, channelled by their own belief in miracles. A perfectly untraceable form of gentle revenge. With that little detour in Portugal out of the way, his next challenge was to find a method of laundering the profits from his American investments in such a way that they could reach him. William Gibbs McAdoo, his New York contact, came up with what seemed like the perfect opportunity. He would cash out all of Saunière's stocks and exchange them for a share in an exciting and expanding new industry: cinema.'

'Saunière and cinema: it doesn't sound right together,' said Ruby.

'The world changes fast. Even ex-priests on the run need to keep up,' said the Templar. 'This is the period shortly after the war when Charlie Chaplin was getting fed up with the restrictions of working for the existing Hollywood studios. He teamed up with Douglas Fairbanks and a couple of others to form their own studio, United Artists. Each of the four artists had a twenty per cent stake in the company. The other fifth was held by the lawyer who put it all together, Mr McAdoo.'

'Did the actors have any idea about Saunière's financial involvement?' asked Ruby.

'As far as they were aware, the lawyer was their other partner. They knew nothing of Saunière's existence, so they couldn't know that McAdoo's shares were his in name only, held on behalf of the priest. Meanwhile Saunière settled in Paris, living off regular dividend cheques from McAdoo, preparing for his eventual journey across the Atlantic. And that would have gone as planned were it not for the arrival of an unexpected visitor at his hotel.'

'Papa!' came a voice from the hallway. Aurelia sprinted into the kitchen, followed by Charlie and Rocco. The Templar creakily raised himself up and Aurelia hugged her father with a passion that caused him to wince. The expression in his eyes betrayed the rarity of such contact.

'My daughter, Aurelia,' said the Templar, almost apologetically.

'These men tracked me to my apartment and followed me here,' she said, pointing at Charlie and Rocco. 'You said they were involved in that crash?'

'It is all right,' said the Templar, disentangling himself from his daughter. 'If our new guests would like to take a seat. We are almost all here. I will ask the American women in to join us.'

He limped to the corridor. While Aurelia, Rocco and Charlie shuffled into the kitchen chairs, Scabies slipped silently out into the barn for an overdue smoke. The Templar returned with Justina and Winnifred. The kitchen now felt crowded. There were not enough seats for everyone, so the American women sat on the tiled counters at the side of the room and the Templar stood against the wall. Scabies' absence went unremarked.

'Perhaps you could wait in the library, Aurelia?' The Templar said. The girl stood up and seemed about to say something to her father. Then, as she stepped towards the exit she glanced back at the group of people in the kitchen and formed the shape of a word with her lips, but then seemed to think better of it and walked to the library in silence. The Templar shut the door behind her and helped himself to the vacated seat.

'Well, I have to admit this has been easier than I was expecting,' he announced. 'All of you together. There is bound to be some sacred symmetry there. Now, where was I?'

'You were about reveal to us the identity of Saunière's unexpected guest chappy in Paris,' prompted Ratty.

'You really want to know?'

'If it's not too much trouble,' said Ratty. 'I think I speak for all of us when I say that satiation of our curiosity is a not unreasonable expectation.'

The Templar seemed to roll his eyes before answering. 'The visitor's name was Lord Ballashiels,' said the Templar.

'My great-great-goodness-knows?'

'And his arrival marked the worst day of Saunière's life. Which brings us to today. The work is almost complete at Stiperstones.'

'What work?' asked Ratty. 'I didn't hire any builders. Can't afford to unless I find Saunière's stash, which now seems less likely than ever.'

'It is not Saunière's stash that we seek,' said the Templar. 'But Saunière himself.'

'Surely the old rogue is pushing up the dandelions by now?'

'His body,' sighed the Templar. 'We seek his remains.'

'I knew it. Well you sure won't find them in Rennes,' said Winnifred. 'I can vouch for that.'

'So you can confirm my family history after all?' pipped Justina, suddenly animated and excited. You've got my DNA sample. When will you compare it with Saunière? Or have you already done it?'

'I will come to that in due course. When Lord Ballashiels called on Saunière in Paris in 1920, he was in no mood for socialising. He threatened the priest. Tore up a letter he had received from Saunière. This letter contained the news that, many years previously, Emma Calvé had borne a son.'

'A son with questionable fatherhood?' asked Ratty.

'Precisely. Accurate paternity tests did not exist in those days. Saunière had reached out to Lord Ballashiels, wishing to establish contact with the young man. Ballashiels was livid at the mere suggestion that he was born of doubtful paternity. Refused even to entertain the possibility that the priest might have been his close relation. Forbade Saunière from entering his life in any way.'

'You mean Saunière might have been Lord Ballashiels' father?' asked Rocco.

'Well, technically,' said Ratty, 'there is only ever one Lord at a time. The boy would have been an Honourable, not an Earl.'

'He is right,' said the Templar.

'Cool,' said Charlie, who hadn't really been following any of this.

'But how would Saunière have fathered a Ballashiels?' asked Ruby. 'Oh, I remember! Your mother mentioned something about your great-great-grandfather having an affair with Emma Calvé. If Calvé had been seeing both men at once she would have had no clue as to the father of the baby.'

'The then Lord Ballashiels claimed the child as his own and took it to England,' the Templar continued. 'He was able to offer a more stable family upbringing than Saunière, who couldn't ever have admitted to being a father – well, not that kind of father, of course. Anyway,

Lord Ballashiels had thought Stiperstones was an environment that would have a greater chance of allowing the baby to grow into a well-rounded young man.'

'Fiddle faddle with knobs on,' said Ratty. 'Utter twiddle twaddle. My great-grandfather was born in 1894. I knew that his father had dallied with a certain Parisian opera star, but there has never been any question in the family archives that this baby was mixed race.'

'Mixed race?' asked Ruby.

'British and French,' he replied. 'Nothing more mixed up than that.'

The Templar ignored the insult. 'Aurelia has organised the destruction of Stiperstones Manor, but don't worry, Lord Ballashiels. It is for a good reason.'

'That young filly is knocking down my home? Is this true? Does she work for Shropshire County Council?'

Aurelia returned to the kitchen.

'I asked you to wait in the library,' said the Templar.

'It's all right, Papa, I can take care of myself. And I can take care of you. I didn't think I should leave you alone with these people.'

'Thank you, Aurelia, but I am just fine.'

'And I think we should tell that weird-looking English man why his home must be demolished,' she added, looking at Ratty, who looked over his shoulder. 'It is only fair.'

The Templar nodded and began speaking. 'Saunière spent more than a decade trying to gain access to Calvé's son, but the young man wanted nothing to do with the priest. His future title and inheritance were at stake. The last thing he wanted to become public knowledge was the possibility that he was descended from a fling between an opera star and a priest. He used expensive and complicated legal tricks to keep Saunière away and to prevent anyone from knowing about the paternity dispute. None of the injunctions had any validity after 1917. How could they? You cannot ban a dead person from coming near you. So things inevitably escalated beyond mere letters. Even though he knew the odds were against him, Saunière travelled to England in 1932, prepared for a final showdown with Lord Ballashiels and to convince his son of what he saw as the truth.'

'But the priest chappy was in Rennes in 1932,' said Ratty. 'That was when he showed his somewhat miserable face in the Chaplin film.'

'That is correct,' answered Aurelia. 'He journeyed to Rennes-le-Château one last time. We don't know if it was for sentimental reasons, or to retrieve something, or to meet his unwitting business partner Charlie Chaplin.'

'Or to send a message,' said Ruby. 'Makes sense. It was his final clue. By appearing on film with Chaplin he's announcing his connection to United Artists. He's making a point. Anyone who followed that link would eventually learn about his twenty per cent holding in the film company. That's his legacy. That's his treasure.'

'Twenty per cent of United Goddamn Artists?' asked Winnifred. 'That's insane. It's got to be worth a billion bucks.'

'A billion dollars!' exclaimed Justina. 'You hear that, everyone? That's why I'm here. That's what all this shit has been for.'

'Now you must understand why it was so important to find Saunière's remains and obtain a DNA match to whoever was his true descendant,' said the Templar. 'Even at the expense of what I am sure is a fine English country house.'

'Not really,' sighed Ratty. 'Something of a wreck, to be honest. Especially after the fire.'

'Ah yes, the fire. Which revealed a body behind the panelling,' said the Templar. 'Do you know who we think that body is?'

'Surely you're not suggesting that my great-grandfather took down the oak panelling, stuffed poor Saunière inside the void and nailed it back up again?'

'He is, Ratty. The pieces all fit,' said Ruby. 'I think he's right. Your great-grandfather must have done it.'

'Never!' cried Ratty.

'How do you know?' she asked.

'Because he would never do a thing like that.'

'Kill a priest?'

'No, I mean he would never faff around with the oak panelling. That would be manual labour. Never in a million wotsnames. But snuffing a sermon-spewer? Well, it's probably not that unusual round our way.'

'Well you might have told us,' said Justina. 'We spent ages trying to dig up his bones for a DNA sample and you had them in your house all along.'

'I must profess to a modicum of surprise at this revelation,' said Ratty.

'But if your DNA turns out to be a match—' began Ruby.

'Then Lord Ballashiels is the true heir to the billion-dollar fortune over which we have been keeping watch all these years,' said the Templar.

'No!' screamed Ratty. 'That would be the most awful and rotten thing that could happen to a chap!'

'Why?' asked Ruby. 'Because you might lose your title? Big deal. You'll be a billionaire. You can buy a hundred titles.'

'It's too high a price to pay,' said Ratty.

'Need I repeat, Ratty, you will be a billionaire!' said Ruby, very slowly.

'But don't you see? No amount of money can change the appalling implication of this.'

'What are you talking about?' asked Ruby. 'What's so appalling about being descended from Saunière and Emma Calvé? If it's true, you will be—'

'French!'

'Oh, Ratty,' she groaned. 'You're already a xenophobic, idiotic, innumerate inbred. I can't see that being French will lessen your worth by any measurable amount.'

'You won't be French, honey,' said Justina, 'because *I* am the descendant of Saunière. Calvé toured America in the 1890s. When she arrived she was already pregnant. She had the baby in the States and gave it up immediately for adoption.'

'Calvé had two babies?' asked Ruby.

'Off the record, yes,' said the Templar. 'That is correct. Each was hushed up for the sake of her career. A scandal would have been disastrous for her.'

The phone rang. Aurelia went to answer it. Those in the kitchen strained to hear her words from the other end of the hallway.

'That will be the police,' said the Templar. 'Quite convenient that they were here a short while ago. I sent them back to Quillan with Lord Ballashiels' DNA sample. They took it straight to the lab for me. The DNA samples from the bones found at Stiperstones and from Justina Saunière are already there. My contacts in the UK have also extracted Ballashiels DNA from the family tomb. I insisted on a sample from someone born before Saunière and Calvé met. I wait for the results with as much anticipation, no doubt, as the rest of you.'

'Is that strictly ethical?' asked Rocco.

'Ethics. You ask about ethics. I am surrounded by tomb robbers, murderers, escaped convicts, trespassers, and who knows what other sorts of criminals you lot are guilty of being,' replied the Templar. 'Does that answer your question?'

Aurelia returned and whispered in his ear. He smiled.
'It appears we have some results.'

**

Scabies flicked the damp stump of his roll-up onto the floor and ground it into the dust with his heel. The pronouncements of the Templar had filtered through to the barn and he had listened with interest while enjoying a smoke without such enjoyment being undermined by reproachful, judgemental looks from Ruby. He put his hand to the door and was about to push it open to re-join the group when he paused.

Something wasn't right.

All this talk of a billion dollar fortune about to be given away. It made no sense. He got the story – that added up – but no one gives away a fortune like that unless the money means nothing to them. This place wasn't bad, as farmhouses went, but it was no palace. Certainly not the abode of anyone to whom a billion dollars was a mere trifle. The Templar was trying hard to come across as everyone's mate, but Scabies wasn't buying it. No one had mentioned his absence, and he resolved to remain in the barn, in earshot but out of sight, until he could be convinced that the Templar was something other than a crook of the greatest magnitude.

**

'Well?' demanded Justina.

Without realising, everyone was leaning forward towards the Templar, eager expectation written deep across their brows.

After a pause that set many pulses quickening, the Templar made an announcement.

'Congratulations are in order,' he said, looking around the room and eventually resting his eyes upon one of the American women. 'Congratulations to you, Justina.'

She pumped her fist into the air and whooped like an ape to which had been returned a long-lost banana.

'Or should I call you, Lady Ballashiels?'

'Huh? What the hell?'

'It seems you are the rightful heir to a title and an English country estate.'

'No shit!' Justina's eyes betrayed the complex mathematics currently crunching through her mind. Was a title and a country house worth more than the Saunière inheritance? Could she exploit this on reality television shows and make money – if not a billion, then at least a few million dollars – that way? What were the tax implications to the IRS? Or would she cease to be a US citizen now that she was an English aristocrat? And could she knock at the door of Buckingham Palace any time she fancied taking tea with the Queen?

'Gosh,' said Ratty, his voice high-pitched and weak. 'It would be discourteous not to warn you that the pile you appear to have inherited is of somewhat negative worth. The debts of the house far exceed its value. For me to step aside from that burden is a not an inconsiderable relief. My sympathies, Your Ladyship.'

'Huh?' she asked. 'You for real?'

'And where does that leave me?' asked Ratty.

The Templar grinned. 'I have also to offer my sincerest congratulations to you, too, *Monsieur* Saunière.'

'No!'

Aurelia passed her father a folder. He brushed the breadcrumbs from the kitchen table and slid the contents of the folder onto it.

'I have here, already prepared, the necessary paperwork,' he informed Ratty, showing him a lavish, typed contract adorned with wax seals, colourful stamps and signatures that included Fairbanks, McAdoo and Chaplin.

'Necessary to do what?'

'To transfer the twenty per cent of United Artists into your name. The shareholding has been held in trust for almost a century. No one has been able to touch it. Only a verified descendant can cash in the shares or bequeath them to someone else. Finally we have the DNA evidence to transfer the shares out of the trust and into your name and control. You may sell them or leave them in your will to others. Our role in this is now ended.'

'Well, I really don't know if I should. I mean this is all so sudden, and I don't know what to think.'

'Ratty, just sign it!' ordered Ruby. 'You're broke. Be rich for once. You might like it.'

The Templar passed a pen to him. Ratty noticed the man's hand was shaking.

'Sign there,' said the Templar, pointing with a wobbly finger. 'And be careful with the document. It's very old and we don't have a copy. Our organisation has guarded it with our lives for generations. Only an original with the irreplaceable signatures of the other four shareholders – including Charlie Chaplin himself – can be used to claim the twenty per cent of the film company and a century of accumulated dividends. Two sets of these documents were produced a century ago. We have this set, the other has been missing for decades.'

'Gosh,' said Ratty. 'Perhaps I should consult a—'

'Ratty!' Ruby snapped.

'Of course. Don't want to delay you all.'

He took the pen and signed the document without reading a word of it.

'Right, all done,' said the Templar.

'That's it?' asked Ratty.

'Yes.'

'And that trifling matter of the billion dollar shareholding?'

'All yours. You now own twenty per cent of United Artists film company.'

'Quite. Golly. That was easy.'

***

Too easy, thought Scabies, peering through the little window as everyone started filing out of the room. When Ratty and the Templar were the only ones left in the kitchen, the Templar closed the door and seemed to lock it. Scabies tensed. This didn't look right.

'There are a few matters I need to discuss with you before you leave,' said the Templar, inviting Ratty to sit once more.

With great care, Ratty placed the share transfer document on the table and sat beside it. 'Of course,' he replied.

'These shares. You own them for as long as you shall live. And if anything should happen to you, the shares, now free of the restrictions of the trust, automatically transfer to the beneficiary named in this document.'

'Beneficiary?' asked Ratty.

'It is merely a temporary measure,' said the Templar. 'It names me as the sole beneficiary should anything happen to you. Once you get home you are welcome to get the document changed and leave it to someone of your choosing.'

'Right. Jolly good,' said Ratty, unsure whether it was really necessary to be detained just to have such a brief codicil explained to him.

'So the only question remaining,' said the Templar, reaching into a cupboard and producing a shotgun that shook noticeably in his hands, is how long will you live?'

Ratty exhaled with a squeak as if he had a deflating balloon wedged in his gullet. 'I say!' he protested. 'Not cricket!'

'An English game. You must forgive my ignorance of the rules.'

'I knew there was a reason not to trust your sort,' said Ratty.

'My sort?'

'French,' said Ratty, ejecting the word as if it were a fly in his mouth.

'You are as French as I am.'

'Never! And besides, I thought we were singing from the same hymn sheet. If you're going to point that frightful device at me I will have seriously to entertain the possibility that we are not even in the same church.'

'If your Frenchness distresses you, fear not,' said the Templar, raising the shotgun and taking aim. 'Your suffering will shortly be over.'

Ratty wished there was something he could do. Wished someone could come to his rescue. Someone streetwise like Scabies. He knew his wishes never came true. Ruby's strictly platonic friendship was proof enough of that, and he prepared to end his life on a note of regret. But his track record on wishes was about to change in a most dramatic manner.

The oil drum thundered into the kitchen like a Catherine Wheel, flames spewing and thrashing as putrid olive oil splattered and ignited. Ratty dived sideways and climbed into the kitchen sink. The drum crashed into the table, pushing it aside, spraying it with oil which then burned with a ferocity that shocked even Scabies. The musician launched his second salvo, another burning drum. This one was aimed directly – by means of a well-practised kick – at the Templar, who had backed himself up against the door, torn between reaching through the flames to try to save the rapidly disappearing United Artists share document and trying to save himself. His indecision removed both options. Charred fragments of the document floated into the air and spread across the room, some landing back in the fierce flames and vanishing, others settling, unrecognisable, upon the green tiles of the counter top.

The Templar dropped his gun and tried to dodge the approaching flaming barrel, but his already injured legs would not move with the degree of rapidity that his mind would have preferred. Flames leapt onto his trousers. He screamed and fell to the floor, writhing and twisting.

'Come on, Ratty!' shouted Scabies. 'This way!'

'Oughtn't we to put him out, first?' asked Ratty, climbing down from the sink and preparing to fill the kettle to pour over the Templar.

'Not with water,' said Scabies, with undisguised reluctance.

'Oh, quite. Yes. Oil-based fire. Should know that by now, I suppose.'

Scabies removed his leather jacket. Ratty likewise. Between them they smothered the Templar's legs and left him steaming and moaning on the floor.

'Fools!' screamed the Templar in a manner which Ratty considered to be most ungrateful. 'All is lost! Without that document the legacy can never be claimed!'

'Easy come, easy go,' said Scabies with a shrug, before dragging the Templar out of the smoke-filled kitchen to the barn.

'Should we leave the fellow here with his olive oil?' asked Ratty.

'Why not. He can fix himself a nice salad,' said Scabies.

***

'I am afraid I have no keys to offer you. Security doesn't seem relevant when the house has a gaping hole in its side where half of it has collapsed. Oh, and you'll have to deal with Mater. She might not take to the idea too easily. Rather stuck in her ways. Might take a modest-sized army to dislodge the old fruit. My accountant will furnish you with a complete list of how much is owed and to whom. Even before half the place burned to the ground, the value of Stiperstones was insufficient to cover its multitudinous debts. I really am most grateful to be free of such a burden and wish you the best of—'

'Keep it.'

Winnifred looked at Justina in approval, saying nothing.

'I beg your wotsits?'

Justina looked into the tired and emotional eyes of His Lordship. 'Keep the house. Keep the title. I don't want it.'

Ratty felt a tear in his eye. He'd been bluffing, of course. A show of gentlemanly indifference to the loss of everything that made him who he was. If she declined to challenge his title, he would keep the house and its liabilities, but more importantly he would remain a Ballashiels. The whole Saunière shadow could evaporate and the sun would once more shine upon him. And it would be a British sun shining on what remained of the dyed hair upon his British head.

'If I may enquire, and, well, it seems to me, I don't know, rather, um—'

'Are you trying to ask why I don't want what's rightfully mine?' Justina asked, hoping to stop Ratty in

- 213 -

his tracks before they both succumbed to the frailty of old age. Before he could reply, she cut him off. 'Then I'll tell you. It has nothing to do with the money. I could make money out of the title, I'm sure. Lady Thingummy has a ring to it, and that could translate into plenty of cash Stateside, but I'm not going to take your title and your home because it's everything you have. It's your life. And what you did to the Templar guy saved his life. And because you saved his life, he's ensured all charges against me and Winnifred are dropped. So we get our lives. I owe it all to you.'

'Gosh. Well, I can't take all the credit. This drummer chappy next to me was somewhat quicker off the mark in the fire damping department. And if he hadn't started the inferno in the first place, I wouldn't be here at all.'

Scabies gave Justina a heroic grin. 'Just doing my job. Any time you need someone to set fire to some drums, call me.'

Ruby entered the corridor.

'How's the Patient doing?' asked Winnifred.

'He's maxed out on morphine,' she said. 'They reset the pins. Surgery went well. He's delirious and talking to Rocco about Charlie Chaplin. The nurse says the rest of you can go and see him in a minute, two at a time, after they've checked his stitches.'

'What is he saying about the Chaplin chappy?' asked Ratty.

'He's talking about when Chaplin's body was kidnapped in Switzerland in the seventies,' she replied. 'When they got him back, they had to bury him in a concrete tomb in case it happened again.'

'Why would it happen again?' asked Justina.

'Because,' said Ruby, 'Chaplin's casket was rumoured to contain items related to Saunière, and Rocco is of the demented opinion that the rumours are true. He's convinced the missing backup documents that would permit the transfer of the billion dollar United Artists shareholding are still inside it. Whoever gets hold of them could still claim Saunière's inheritance. Which is stupid and irrelevant because they've put him in a theft-proof grave. Only the world's best tunneller would have a hope of getting that prize.'

Winnifred's face seemed to light up. 'So Chaplin's still buried in Switzerland?' she asked, standing up. 'No one's tried to rob the grave site since the seventies?'

Justina also seemed to stretch her legs ready to stand. Ratty gave a yawn and elongated his frame. Charlie and Scabies fidgeted.

'That's what the Patient and Rocco were saying,' said Ruby. 'Ask Rocco yourself.'

Ruby poked her head back into the ward and looked in the direction of the Patient's bed. Rocco was gone. When she turned back to the corridor, Winnifred, Justina, Scabies, Charlie and Ratty were nowhere to be seen.

Proudly published by Accent Press

www.accentpress.co.uk